Hunted

A Marine Raiders Romance

Allyson Charles

Contents

Chapter One

A STORM WAS COMING. Jake Skinner tipped his beer back and scanned the bar. No one stood out. Everything was in its place. Still, he felt it. A storm was coming. He just didn't know what form it would take.

"Relax, man." Travis Kowalski, one of the members of his five-man squad, clapped his shoulder. "You've been as jumpy as a virgin at an orgy all night. There aren't any threats at *The Limber Ginger*. You're scoping the place out like you expect insurgents to attack at any moment."

Jake pressed his lips together. He was *trying* to relax. He had that itch, however. The one he got when things were about to go tits up.

Ryan Kelly, another member of their elite squad of Marine Raiders, strolled across the room, pausing to say hello to a couple of co-eds along the way. When he reached them, he rested his elbows on the bar next to Jake and ordered a beer. "This place is hopping tonight. A room full of willing women and you two are standing here just watching. What gives?"

"Psych has another one of his feelings." Travis shrugged at Jake's look. "What? We can always tell when you get a premonition. I think you're off-base tonight. Nothing is going to go sideways at *The Limber Ginger*."

Jake grunted. Travis wasn't wrong. There was nothing threatening here, unless you counted the drunk at the dart boards. But he hadn't been given the call sign Psych, short for Psychic, for nothing. His intuition had saved their asses on more than one occasion. Trouble was coming.

He tried to shake off his wariness. "What are you doing back here?" he asked Ryan. "You left with that blonde an hour ago."

Ryan took his mug from the bartender, giving the woman a lazy smile. "We had fun. Then she got chatty."

Travis snorted. "Asking for the phone number of the guy who just screwed her isn't being chatty. It's called being a normal woman."

Ryan lifted his beer to his mouth. "Asshole," he muttered.

"Manwhore," Travis responded good-naturedly.

Jake shook his head. The way his men bickered they could have been married. He checked his watch. "We have to be at the beach at oh-five-hundred for training," he said. As Element Leader of the

Second Marine Raider Battalion's Alpha Squad, it sometimes felt like his role was to act as his men's scheduling assistants, reminding them when and where they had to be. But once they were on the job, their focus was unparalleled.

Ryan smirked. "Does someone need his beauty sleep? You're getting old, man, if pleasing one of these ladies will take too much out of you."

"I can please the ladies just fine." Jake narrowed his eyes. He was thirty-three, damn it. In his prime. But when a man hit thirty, he started thinking more with his big head. And losing sleep over a woman you'd never see again just didn't hold the same thrill.

He rolled his shoulders. None of his men were looking for anything serious. In their line of work, serious wasn't easy to come by. As a member of a Special Operations Force, their military service was a bit different than most others, When a call came in, they could be deployed from a couple of days to a couple of months, leaving without notice and without being able to tell their friends and family back home where they wcre going. Not great for relationships.

Still, one-night stands just didn't hold the same appeal.

A tray full of bottles crashed to the floor. Jake's gaze snapped to the blushing waitress standing over the mess. She dropped to her knees to clean it up, and Travis hurried to her to help. The owner, a large man with a bushy red beard strolled over and handed Travis a towel. He threw back his head and hooted at something Travis said.

Jake tapped his fingers on the bar, his jittery feeling growing. He drained his beer and debated getting another. Oh-five-hundred wasn't far away, but realistically it wasn't a bad thing for him and his men to train on little sleep. When they were out in the field, shut-eye was hard to come by. It was better to train under those conditions now, when there were safety precautions in place.

No, it wasn't fatigue that worried him.

A waitress they knew sashayed up to give the bartender an order. Ryan leaned down and murmured something in her ear, causing her eyes to light up.

"Thirty minutes 'til I'm off," she said.

Ryan gave her a wicked smile. "I'll be counting the seconds."

Another waitress paused in her rounds. "You shouldn't date guys from Camp LeJeune, Amita." She glared at Ryan. "That's a lesson I only had to learn once."

Jake chuckled. "*She's* got your number."

Amita looked uncertain. She picked up her tray. "I have to go deliver these drinks." Turning, she hurried to a corner table.

Ryan gave a low whistle. "I do hate being stereotyped."

"Especially when the stereotype fits." Travis sank back onto his stool, his lips twitching. The bar owner was a step behind him.

"You're breaking me heart." Kieran Kennedy said in a thick Irish brogue. He ran his hand over his beard. His large belly strained against the buttons of his shirt. "I do so want my niece to marry a nice, Irish boy, Kelly, but I fear you might not be the one for her. I can't have the girl ending up with a dog."

"This mythical niece that we hear about all the time but have never seen?" Travis raised an eyebrow. "Admit it, Kennedy. You made her up. Appearing like a doting uncle gives you a leg up with the ladies."

Kieran slapped his towel on the bar. "You're all hopeless. Me making up my niece," he muttered.

Amita sidled up to Ryan, clasping her empty tray to her stomach. "Another girl said she'd cover the rest of my shift. I'm ready to go whenever you are."

Kieran rolled his eyes. "Jesus, Mary, and Joseph. I've created a den of iniquity." He shuffled away, shaking his head.

Ryan held out his arm. "My chariot of iniquity awaits."

Amita giggled, tossed the tray on the bar, and threaded her arm through Ryan's.

"Oh-five-hundred," Jake shouted the reminder to his retreating back.

Ryan waved his fingers but kept moving.

Jake rubbed the back of his neck. He watched them leave through the front door, then eyed the rear exit again, then the door to the kitchen. Still no threats.

"Still have that feeling, huh?" Travis signaled the bartender for his tab. "You think something's going to go wrong on our next mission?"

Jake forced his shoulders to relax. If his team thought he was edgy, they'd get edgy too. "Just tired." He dipped his chin and gave him a look. "It's exhausting having to haul your sorry asses over walls all day." The obstacle course they'd trained on that afternoon had been fun as hell, but it was as good an excuse as any.

Travis huffed a laugh. "You keep telling yourself that's the reason you're exhausted. It couldn't be that you have a birthday coming up next month and you're starting to feel the years."

Jake narrowed his eyes. He wasn't a step slower than Chris Gunn, the youngest member of their squad, but the reminder of his birthday still stung. He knew he couldn't be a Raider forever, but he wanted to work alongside his men as long as possible. Serving his country, helping those in need, it was the best job in the world.

But it couldn't last forever.

He gratefully took the beer the bartender gave him. It was his second, and final, one. He looked at his watch again. If he drank fast, he could be in bed before midnight.

"Happy Birthday," the bartender said. She gave him a flirty smile and leaned forward, giving him an excellent view of her cleavage.

Jake tipped his beer at her, his smile tight. It had to be the twitchy feeling he was having why his dick showed zero interest in the woman. It couldn't have anything to do with his age.

It was ironic. Getting laid would probably help settle his nerves. He dropped his gaze to the bartender's ass as he chugged back some beer. Nope. Still nothing.

"You taking leave to visit family for your birthday?" Travis asked.

Jake shook his head. His parents had been asking when he was going to come home again. It had been awhile since his last visit and he had leave coming, but the thought of getting out of town right now didn't sit right.

He gripped the back of his neck and growled. That itch between his shoulder blades was growing. He just couldn't shake the feeling that something was coming. Something big.

And he needed to be here for it.

Chapter Two

As BAD DECISIONS WENT, this one came with some definite perks. The view of the ocean at sunset was amazing. The yacht was beautiful. Her gin and tonic was ice cold. It was only the company that was lacking.

Caroline Carter rested her forearms on the railing of the yacht, her shoulders slumping. None of the perks mattered. She wished she was anywhere but here.

She never should have come on this date with a man who was a virtual stranger. She knew better. But instead, she'd listened to that little voice inside, the one that sounded suspiciously like her best friend, Sam, and decided to say, 'what the hell,' for once in her life. To be spontaneous. So when Brent the stockbroker had hit on her in her favorite restaurant, inviting her to a party on a yacht with some friends of his, she'd said yes. Decided to let her hair down and have a little fun.

And, oh boy, was she having fun.

Not.

She glanced over her shoulder at the three women lounging by the pool in string bikinis. At the other end of the deck, a surly man stood with his arms over his chest, his eyes hidden by sunglasses.

She'd tried to start a conversation with the other women, but she suspected from the blank looks they'd given her that they didn't speak English. Either that, or they were just rude. Or snobs. The tiny scraps of fabric they wore probably cost more than her mortgage payment.

The men on board were even less friendly, not even deigning to give her a nod.

Caroline turned back around and faced the ocean off the North Carolina coast. The sun was a ball of watery oranges and tangerines, sinking over the purpling coastline. As pretty as the scene was, she was never going out with Brent again.

They'd met at the Hacienda Bar and Grill. She and Sam had been eating lunch together when Sam had gotten an emergency call from her little sister and run out halfway through the meal. And while Caroline had been finishing hers up, Brent had come over and asked to join her for a drink. He'd been charming, if a bit oily, and it had been a long time since she'd enjoyed a man's company.

She gripped the railing. It wasn't just any man's company she yearned for, though; it was the *right* man's company. And Brent wasn't that man. He tried too hard to impress. From the gleam in his eyes, he obviously thought taking a woman on a jaw-dropping yacht was enough to get in her pants. His hand had crept lower and lower down her back as he pointed out every feature of the boat. She snorted. A boat that wasn't even his.

After taking her on the grand tour, he'd ditched her up on deck. Leaving her alone with strangers was a sure way to not get a second date.

These past couple of years, all she'd felt was alone.

She turned and hooked her elbows on the railing. Frowning, she scanned the interior of the yacht visible through the floor-to-ceiling glass wall. The men who'd been there before had disappeared. Brent was nowhere in sight. He might not be her soulmate, but she was bored, and he was better than nothing.

A gust of wind blew a hank of her pale hair across her face as she marched across the deck to find him. Now that the sun was going down, her cotton Capri pants and tank top weren't doing their job keeping her warm. If this boat wasn't going to turn around soon, she at least hoped there'd be a spare jacket for her to wear.

Pressing open the glass door, she strode down a short hallway and peeked in the room at the rear of the boat. Empty.

She took the stairs down a level and followed the voices she heard. The heels of her sandals sank into the red velvet carpet with each step. She stopped at the edge of a doorway and bit her lip. Brent was in there, but he didn't sound happy. He was speaking Spanish, something Caroline hadn't thought the preppy frat boy would be able to do. She was slightly impressed. Not enough to extend this date, though.

Another man laughed, the sound grating.

Caroline peeked around the door and froze. Even her lungs stopped working. In her two years of college, she hadn't done a lot of partying, but she could recognize the package that sat on the glass-topped desk. Brick shaped and wrapped in foil, the block of cocaine was something she recognized from every cop movie and TV show she'd ever seen.

Brent stood in front of a desk, a black duffel bag gripped in one hand. The edge of another brick imprinted on the fabric from the inside. The man behind the desk had one booted foot up on the glass top. His greased black hair gleamed under the lights.

She pressed her back against the wall, her chest heaving. Nausea spiked so hard in her stomach she went light-headed. This was what she got for being spontaneous. For going against every rule she'd ever learned about letting a stranger take her somewhere isolated. She'd always thought it would be an abandoned warehouse or a creepy panel van she'd have to steer clear of, not a multi-million dollar yacht. Live and learn.

She prayed she'd live long enough to learn.

The boat rolled with a swell, right along with her stomach. Caroline lifted her foot to tiptoe away, and the boat jerked sideways with the next wave. She stumbled.

Right into the open doorway.

The man behind the desk looked up, his eyes narrowing.

She snapped backwards, as though his gaze was a blow. "Sorry." She held up her hands. "I was just looking for Brent. I didn't see anything."

Damn. Why had she said that? A person would only say that if they *had* seen something. And it was obviously a lie, anyway. She was standing five feet away. Of course, she'd seen something.

Brent spun to face her. He smoothed a hand down his white linen jacket. "Caroline. It's not what it looks like."

The man behind the desk snapped his gaze to Brent, his dark brows drawing low.

"Of course not." She took a step back. She smiled, but knew it looked more crazed than friendly. "Everything's fine."

"Get her." The seated man's nostrils flared.

That...didn't sound like it would end well for her. Heart rabbiting in her chest, she forced her feet to move just as fast. She tore down the hallway.

Brent called out from behind. "Caroline! Stop!"

She almost laughed, but it came out more a whimper. She took the stairs two at a time and flung herself out the door, earning curious glances from the women in the pool.

And the man standing guard. He pressed his finger to his ear, tilting his head, then said something in a low voice. He started circling the pool towards her.

Caroline spun, stumbled on a pool floatie, and raced down the outer walkway.

Brent called her name again, louder now.

Dammit, dammit, dammit. Why did he have to take her on a boat? There was nowhere to run. She hit the rear of the boat—Aft? Stern? She shook her head. Now was not the time to care about nautical terminology!—and looked wildly about. Night had almost fallen, but lights in the ceiling of the yacht let her see shapes in the gray. She searched for a weapon, a lifeboat, anything that could save her.

"Caroline." Brent held his hands up in front of him and stepped carefully forward. "It's not what you think."

"You're not dealing drugs?" Her heart thumped so hard against her ribs they hurt.

The guard from the pool rounded the corner, followed by the man Brent had been talking to in the office.

He glared at Brent. "Tell me you didn't bring a woman on my yacht who isn't already involved with your business."

"I just met him today," Caroline whispered.

The guard reached into the front of his jacket and rested his hand on a wedge of black plastic. The butt of a gun.

White lights sparked behind Caroline's eyes. She gripped the back railing.

"Don't be that way, Diaz," Brent whined. "She'll be cool."

Caroline's head bobbed up and down. She could be as cool as the Arctic.

"I don't like carelessness," Diaz said. He nodded to the guard.

The man pulled the gun free from his holster and shot Brent in the back of the head.

Something wet and sticky struck her cheek. Her brain blanked, not wanting to recognize what it could be. Her ears rang. She stared at the gun as it rose from pointing at Brent's prone body to her.

Oh God. Shit. She was about to die. Her legs shook. She might have wet herself. Her body felt so strange all over, it was hard to tell.

The shooter aimed at her head.

Without thought, she flung herself backwards, let gravity take her over the railing.

Another shot rang out a second before she was swallowed by the sea.

Chapter Three

JAKE SUCKED IN A deep breath, inhaling the salty air. The sun was barely over the watery horizon, but he and his men had already put in a five-mile run on the beach. Sweat trickled down his cheek, and he wiped it away with the sleeve of his second-skin compression shirt.

They'd run just enough to get their body temperature up. And now it was time for a cooldown. "How about a bet?" he said. "Last one back to shore buys the next round."

"Sweet." Tony Garcia, the Navy corpsman of their squad, jerked his head at Travis. "Skee is buying tonight."

The rest of the men laughed.

Chris Gunn, the fifth and final member of their squad, clapped Travis on the back. "If you lose again, I promise to get you that set of pink floaties we saw at the store the other day. You can match with our Captain's granddaughter."

Travis planted his hands on his lean hips. "I swear, if you give me floaties, I will shove them so far up your—"

Jake tuned the banter out, rolling his neck. He still had that damn itch between his shoulder blades. He gazed out to sea. He needed to get his head on straight. A mission could be only days away. Maybe that's what his internal warning system was trying to tell him. That things were about to go FUBAR on their next op.

He buried that disturbing thought. They trained hard, preparing themselves for any eventuality. They'd be fine.

"Let's go," he said. Jake ran a few steps into the surf, then dove into the next low swell. The bite of cold was exhilarating to his system, his shirt's thin layer of neoprene doing little to blunt the shock. His arms sliced through the water as they headed out to sea for their three mile swim.

The sounds of gulls looking for their breakfast faded away until he only heard his steady breathing and the lap of water against his body. His lungs strained, but he pushed harder.

Their turning point was the Coast Guard's navigational buoy, and Jake wanted to be the first one there. Tony was their fastest swimmer, but he didn't usually swim balls to the walls unless he needed to.

Anticipation drew Jake forward, urged him on. The buoy bobbed in the waves, clinking metallically.

Jake lifted his head. It was close, only fifty or so yards away. The blue light at the top flashed dimly in the early morning light.

He drew up, treading water.

Tony stopped by his side. "What's wrong? You have a cramp?"

Jake rubbed his eyes and looked again. His lungs stalled. "Holy shit." He plunged back into the water and swam hard.

It hadn't been a seal he'd seen laying on the buoy. The animal that was currently curled on top of the large, metal beacon was much too pale to be anything other than human.

Shouts rose behind him, and Jake knew his men had seen the figure, as well. He reached the buoy and hauled himself halfway out of the water.

The woman had wrapped herself around the vertical superstructure like a snake. She'd obviously been holding on for dear life, and something in Jake's heart tore. Whoever the woman was, she'd had one hell of a time.

He took her wrist, only taking a full breath when he felt the faintest of flutters beneath his fingers. "She's alive," he yelled to his men. How long she'd stay so was anyone's guess, however. Her skin was ice cold. She needed medical attention and they were a mile and a half out in the Atlantic.

Ryan pulled himself partially out of the water on the other side of the buoy. "Are we bringing her back in?"

Jake shook his head. He climbed the rest of the way up and sat on the edge of the flotation section, his feet dangling in the water. He grabbed the bottom of his shirt and tore it up and over his head, tossing it into the water. "She's too cold. I don't know if she'd survive more time in the ocean."

As carefully as he could, he lifted the woman onto his lap. She wore nothing but a bra and panties, and Jake pressed as much of his bare skin against hers as he could. He had nothing but his own body heat to warm her.

"Viper, Skee, haul ass to shore and get a rescue boat out here."

Tony hesitated, treading water. "Be careful you don't lose too much of your own body heat." He frowned. "People have died trying to warm up others that way."

Christ. Tony was their primary medic, but they didn't have time for a medical lecture. "Go."

Tony nodded before he and Travis turned for shore.

Jake pushed the woman's hair from her face. It had mostly dried, and was the pale blond color usually only seen on children. Her eyes remained closed, but she tucked her head close to his chest.

Jake's heart did a weird flip.

She was beautiful, yes, with a wide mouth and high cheekbones and a cute turned-up nose, but it was the sense of familiarity that struck him. Like he'd grown up knowing this woman even though he was certain he'd never seen her before.

Every protective instinct Jake possessed flared to life. How the hell had she ended up here?

He looked for bruises and thankfully saw none.

"What do you think?" Chris, usually the most easy-going guy in their group, looked deadly serious. "Accident or intentional?"

Jake drew the woman closer, arranging her legs over his lap. He chafed the skin on her back, her thighs, anywhere he could reach. "I think she had a very bad night however the hell she ended up here."

The woman moaned. She turned into Jake, burying her nose at his throat.

Jake cradled the back of her head. "Sweetheart, can you wake up?" He skimmed his palm up and down her side. "Open those eyes. Let me see that you're okay."

She mumbled something indistinct and shifted.

"Come on now," he said in a coaxing voice. "Time to wake up. You have to let me know that you're okay." His heart pounded sluggishly. She needed to be okay. He'd rescued countless people before, did his best to ensure no harm came to anyone. At least, anyone who didn't deserve it. But something about the woman curled up on his lap was different.

She was different.

Jake just wasn't quite sure how.

She pressed herself closer, the ice of her skin leaching into his chest.

He'd take it. If he could take all the cold from her, exchange it with his heat, he would.

Her eyelids fluttered. With what looked like immense effort, she finally opened them a crack. Pale blue eyes met his.

She blinked, looked at the ocean, then back at him. Her heart thumped against his chest.

He rubbed her back. "You're okay. You're safe," he murmured. "Can you tell me your name?"

She opened her mouth, but only a harsh rasp came out. His gut clenched as she licked her lips, swallowed, and tried again.

"Caroline," she whispered.

Jake scanned the water. Where was that damn rescue boat? She needed water, and he hated that he couldn't provide it to her.

He looked back down into her sweet face. "Okay, Caroline. We're getting a boat out here to take you to the hospital. You're going to be fine. Do you understand?"

She nodded, then closed her eyes as though that small movement had exhausted her.

"Caroline." He shook her. There was no response. "God damn it."

"They'll be here soon," Ryan said. "She just needs to hang on a little longer."

But soon wasn't good enough. Every minute that passed felt like an hour. Tony and Travis would put everything they had into getting to shore and to help as fast as possible, but the wait still killed him.

Finally, *finally*, the low thrum of an engine reached his ears. A speedboat with Harbor Patrol markings bounced across the swells, heading their way. Two familiar figures stood at the bow.

The pilot cut the engine when he got close, and the boat drifted toward the buoy. Tony tossed a rope to Ryan, and they pulled in close.

Reluctantly, Jake transferred Caroline to Travis when he leaned over the rail, then pulled himself onto the boat after her. "She needs fluids and heat," he said as he took her back into his arms. "Is there an ambulance waiting at the dock?"

The pilot nodded. He waited for all the men to climb onboard then disappeared back into the wheelhouse. The other Harbor Patrol agent un-zipped a bright orange duffel and pulled out a silver emergency blanket. He unfolded it and handed it to Jake.

He wrapped the blanket around Caroline's body then sat down on the bench, holding her close again.

Tony dug through the medical kit and came out with a bag of saline. "There's an IV line." He looked to Jake. "Do you want it here or wait for the EMS?"

"Now." Jake slid the blanket off Caroline's arm.

Tony cleaned a patch of skin with an alcohol wipe, inserted the needle, and taped it to her arm. He held the saline bag in his hand and gently squeezed.

Caroline whimpered, and Jake tried to soothe her. She opened her eyes again, gazed up at him. The creases in her forehead disappeared, her face relaxing.

The trust in her eyes slayed Jake. She didn't know him, had no reason to place her confidence in him, but she nestled into his arms like she knew he would protect her with his life.

His chest expanded. "You're doing great, sweetheart."

She swallowed then winced.

"Water." He didn't look to see who handed him the plastic bottle. He held the water to Caroline's lips and slowly tilted it up.

She greedily sucked the liquid down. The look of betrayal she shot Jake when he took the bottle away almost had him laughing. Her face was so expressive, her spirit seemingly undiminished by her ordeal.

"You can't drink too much at one time," he told her. At her continued scowl, he relented and gave her a tiny sip more. He put the bottle down. "Caroline. Sweetheart." He dragged his thumb over her bottom lip, catching a stray drop of water. "Can you tell me what happened?"

Her gaze clouded. She turned into him and rested her hand on his abdomen.

He ignored how good it felt to have her hand on his bare skin. "Caroline?" he said, but her eyes were already beginning to close, her body relaxing into sleep.

He gave her a tiny shake. "Caroline, what happened to you?"

She blinked open her eyes once more before exhaustion dragged them closed.

Jake bent over her as she mumbled, barely catching her words.

"He tried to kill me," she whispered.

Jake looked at Tony, meeting his narrowed gaze. His friend's jaw went hard, his nostrils flaring. He'd heard her words, as well, and if there was one thing his squad wouldn't stand for, it was a man hurting a woman.

Jake leaned back against the rail as the boat sped towards the marina. The itch between his shoulder blades was finally gone. He looked down at the woman in his arms. Now he knew what his intuition had been trying to tell him.

Trouble had been coming.

And it had landed in his lap in the form of a woman.

Chapter Four

CAROLINE WOKE WITH A start. The white ceiling panels above her were unfamiliar, and her pulse raced as she tried to orient herself.

"Hey," a deep voice beside her said. "You're safe."

She blinked at the man. Cropped, dark brown hair capped a face with a strong jaw and straight nose. Mesmerizing jade green eyes gazed at her steadily, and the tension eased from her body.

It was the man from before. The one who'd rescued her from....

She closed her eyes, but the memories wouldn't go away. Brent. Diaz. The endless depths beneath her as she'd swum and swum, never believing she'd survive the night.

A hand, warm and calloused, covered hers. "Are you hurting anywhere? Do you want me to call for a doctor?"

"No, I'm fine." Her throat hurt. Her voice was raspy. And every muscle in her body ached. But she was alive. She looked into the man's eyes. They really were extraordinary, the color seeming to glow, like sea glass. He wore jeans and a T-shirt and looked solid and steady. "I know you told me your name last night in the ambulance," she said. "But..."

"Jake Skinner." His voice rolled over her like warm honey.

"You saved me," she said, disbelieving. It seemed like a dream, him finding her in the middle of the ocean.

He grinned, tiny wrinkles crinkling the edges of his eyes. "At your service, ma'am."

Her heart pinched. The short hair. The bulging muscles. The ma'am. It all spelled one thing. "You're military."

He nodded. "A Staff Sergeant in the Marines. I know you talked to the police last night," he began.

A harsh chuckle left her throat.

Jake stretched for the pink plastic cup on the side table and poured some water into it. He plopped a straw in the cup and held it up to her mouth.

Gratefully, she took a sip. "I didn't have much I could tell them," she said. "I just had one name. And Brent is...." Her voice trailed off.

"You don't have to talk if you don't want." He scooted his chair closer. "I'm just sorry you had to go through that." A small muscle in his jaw ticked. He looked angry, lethal, and Caroline smiled. It had been a long time since someone had been outraged on her behalf.

"So the cops haven't found that Diaz yet?" she guessed.

He shook his head. "Negative. I know they're going to want to talk to you again. See if you remembered anything more."

"But I haven't." Careful of the IV above her wrist, she rubbed her forehead. "I met Brent at lunch and agreed to go to a party with him. I saw him with Diaz and the drugs, and then I was running."

He stroked his thumb along the back of her hand while he placed the water cup down on the table. He left his hand covering hers, and the slight weight of it soothed her enough to be able to relive the events of the night before, trying to remember something new.

She sucked in a deep breath. "It was so sudden. One moment Brent was standing there, alive, and the next, he was dead. In the movies you at least have a warning, dramatic music or something to let you know what's about to happen." A shiver raced through her body. "My mind just couldn't catch up to what had happened."

"You were in shock. That's normal," Jake said. "It was something you never should have seen." He pressed his lips flat. "Do you make a habit of going onto boats with men you've just met? I don't want to give you a hard time after the night you've had, but that wasn't smart."

She grimaced. "It was very out of character. Just once I wanted to be impulsive, you know? I work in a cubicle at the most boring job at Goldstar Actuarial Company. My most exciting Friday night in the past month was when my internet went out and I shared a piece of pie with the repairman who came out to fix it." She shrugged. "I wanted to have some fun. Trust me, it won't happen again."

"I didn't mean you shouldn't have fun," he said. "But a woman has to be careful."

She eyed his broad shoulders and muscled arms. His biceps were as big as her thigh. "And you don't, I suppose."

He smiled. "I'm careful. Me and my men, we train constantly so we're always prepared."

"Your men?" she said.

He hesitated. "I'm the element leader for my squad in the Second Marine Raider Battalion."

She tilted her head to the side. "Raider Battalion?"

"Special forces, a part of Marine Special Operations Command, or MARSOC, for short."

"Special forces. So you're like a SEAL."

Jake smirked. "Close, except we don't seek out glory like the frogmen do."

She bit her bottom lip. "I've never heard of a Raider before." And she lived next door to a Marine base. Either they were super-secret, or she was super uninformed. Maybe a bit of both. She tended to ignore anything military related.

"Not surprising. Like I said, we keep a low profile." He leaned forward. "The Raiders only formed in 2014, but make no mistake, we're just as well trained as any other special forces division. In fact, we were doing PT when we found you."

He swallowed, his throat rippling. "Finding you on that buoy...." He shook his head. "I talked to the cops. They're going to have officers driving by your home on a regular basis, but as Brent, or Diaz, never knew your last name, they don't think you're in any danger. You didn't tell them your last name, correct?"

She shook her head. "I thought it was more fun remaining mysterious." She groaned. "God, what an idiot I was."

"Like I said, there's nothing wrong with having a bit of fun." His eyes twinkled. "You just need to make sure it's with the right man next time."

The look he gave her made her skin tingle. It wasn't demanding, nor possessive, not quite. She knew he didn't have any expectations, but the heated look held weight all the same.

A weight she didn't want to acknowledge. She couldn't let her attraction to the man develop into anything.

She gave him a tight smile and pushed her blanket back.

"Going somewhere?" he asked.

Caroline's cheeks heated. "I just want to get up and stretch my legs." As she sat up, the pressure in her bladder increased. *And get to the bathroom*. She swung her legs over the edge and stood. The room spiraled, and she blinked.

"Whoa." Jake placed his hands on her shoulders and pressed her back to sitting. "Take it easy. You were severely dehydrated when you were admitted. You need rest."

The world around her steadied, Jake's concerned face becoming clear.

"I'm okay," she said. "I just need to move slower."

"You need to stay in bed." The words combined with the sexy gravel of his voice gave her all sorts of inappropriate thoughts. He was the type of man she wouldn't mind staying in bed with. Except for his one fatal flaw.

She pressed her thighs together. "I'm fine." She pushed against his hands.

They didn't budge.

"Jake, please, I need to get up."

A small divot formed between his eyebrows. "If you need something, I'll bring it to you."

She groaned. "Look, I really need to pee, all right? And while my legs still work I'm not going to do it in a bed pan. Do you understand?"

His lips twitched. "Yes, ma'am." He helped her stand then walked her to the bathroom door, pulling the rolling IV next to him.

"Thanks, I've got it from here," she said at the door.

"Are you sure?" He scanned the bathroom like he thought an enemy might leap at her from behind the toilet at any moment.

Her face flamed hotter. This man had rescued her, seen her in nothing but her underwear, seen her at her absolute worst, but that didn't mean she was going to let him help her pee. "Positive."

"Okay." He took a step back. "Keep the door cracked in case you need help."

She gave him a look as she stepped inside. "I won't need help."

He rested his hand over the doorframe and leaned down to look her in the eye. "Humor me."

Caroline fiddled with the edge of her gown. "I really would like a sound barrier. I'll leave it cracked only if you sing."

He chuckled, the sound rich and throaty. "You've already been through one trauma. You don't need to hear me sing, sweetheart." He pulled the door closed until only a sliver of space remained. "But I'll make a phone call if it will make you feel more comfortable."

She took care of business listening to his low murmurs on the other side of the door. When she looked in the mirror over the sink, she blinked in horror at her reflection. Her hair was a knotted mess, looking brittle from her swim in salt water.

Her lips were cracked, and purplish bruises marred the skin beneath her eyes. In short, she looked like hell.

But she was alive.

She washed her hands then shuffled into the hospital room just as Jake was ending his call.

"How long do I have to stay here?" she asked.

He placed his hand on her lower back and guided her back to bed, pulling the blanket over her as she settled. "I'll get a doctor in here to talk to you, but I can't imagine you'll be here much longer. I'd be happy to drive you home." He frowned. "Though I don't like the thought of you being alone. Do you have anyone to stay with? If not, I could—"

Her best friend, Sam, swept into the room, a worried expression in her chocolate eyes. "I came as soon as I could get off work." She leaned over and enveloped Caroline in a hug. "I can't believe you almost died, CeCe." Pulling back, she ran her gaze over Caroline's body, looking relieved when she saw her all in one piece. Then she turned her attention on Jake.

Caroline made the introductions.

"CeCe?" Jake asked.

"Because my first and last names start with C's," Caroline explained. "Though Sam usually only calls me that when she's angry at me."

"Or freaking out over you. God, someone tried to *kill* you." Sam tucked her shoulder-length brown hair behind an ear. She heaved a sigh. "When do you bust out of this joint?"

"As soon as the doctor gets here, I'm going to ask about being discharged." Caroline fingered her own hair. "I can't wait to take a shower."

Jake crossed his arms over his chest. "Again I don't think you should be alone. I know the police are going to patrol your neighborhood but—"

"She won't be alone," Sam interrupted. "I'll take care of her. It's going to be girls' night for the foreseeable future." She waggled her eyebrows, then frowned. "You can drink, right? Being stranded at sea doesn't mean you can't have alcohol, I hope."

Jake looked heavenward, and Caroline grinned. Her friend made the best margaritas. It would be great having Sam at her house, though she had to admit, she was curious what Jake had been about to offer. There was no way he was going to suggest he stay with her, was there? They'd just met, after all.

The image of Jake in her house, her space, had its appeal. He was so very masculine, and his presence in a house that had only had women living in it for many, many years would be an interesting observation on contradictions.

She squared her shoulders. But that would have led to her having silly romantic notions, and since he was military, they were notions she wouldn't allow herself to pursue.

She was better off not knowing what he'd been about to say.

Jake pinned her with his gaze. "Are you okay with this?" he asked Caroline. "Do you want Sam to stay with you? No offense," he added as Sam planted her hands on her hips, "but if Caroline would be more comfortable with—"

"Sam will be great," Caroline said. And harmless. She wouldn't do anything stupid with Sam staying with her. She might with Jake, however. "Like you said, Diaz doesn't know my last name. He doesn't know how Brent and I met. I'll be fine."

"All right," Jake said, but he didn't look happy. "What's your phone number?"

Automatically, Caroline gave it to him. "But my phone is in the bottom of the ocean. It might take me a while to get a new one."

"Get a new one today." Jake turned to Sam. "Can you help her with that? It's important for security purposes."

"On it." Sam whipped out her own phone and started scrolling, searching for stores they could buy one at, no doubt.

"Keep your old number," Jake said. "I'll text you later so you'll have mine. Call me anytime if you think there's a problem."

Caroline's stomach twisted uneasily. "Do you think there's going to be a problem?" Once she'd been pulled from the water, she'd thought that was it, that her troubles were over. She hadn't thought ahead to the possibility that Diaz might still want her dead. That he might be able to find her.

Jake's shoulders unbunched. He reached over and squeezed her hand.

Her heart rate evened out. This man was like catnip to her, his slightest touch a soothing balm.

She would have to be extra careful around him.

"No, sweetheart. I think you're safe. But I want you to have my number, just in case. All right?"

She nodded, adding the flutters his calling her 'sweetheart' put in her stomach to her mental list of things she needed to ignore. Contacting him would be so tempting, but she would have to resist the urge. The man had saved her life. He probably felt some misplaced duty toward her. But nothing good could come from getting to know him better. Not when she already knew they could be nothing more than friends.

He gathered a windbreaker from the back of his chair, and her palms went damp. She felt safe in his presence, and as much as she loved Sam, her friend just didn't make her feel the same way.

Which was stupid. She couldn't have a Marine, a Raider, at her side at all times. She had to learn how to move on from last night's terror on her own.

"I don't remember if I said it before, but thank you. For rescuing me."

Their gazes locked.

"Anytime," he said, with a sincerity she felt all the way to her bones.

Jake bent down and brushed his lips over her forehead. "I'll see you later."

The rational side of Caroline's brain knew that was a promise she didn't want him to keep. That it would be better to just move on, and never think of him again.

She watched as he strode from her room, her eyes dropping from his wide shoulders to his narrow waist and fine ass.

But the other side of Caroline, the one that dreamt and hungered, well, it wanted something else altogether.

Chapter Five

Jake lasered his gaze through the scope. He slowly exhaled and squeezed the trigger, the MK 18 jerking against his shoulder.

Tony peered through a pair of binoculars next to him as Jake removed his ear protection. "Nice shot," he said.

Jake grunted. When the target was stationary, the shots were easy. Next week they and the other tactical squad that made up their Marine Special Operations Team would be running live scenarios. That was when the fun began.

They had a bet with Delta squad over who would have the best scores. Jake and his men weren't about to lose.

"Have you heard anything about when we might be sent out?" Tony asked.

Ryan, Chris, and Travis looked up from where they were packing their own weapons, curiosity on each of their faces. It had been almost a month since they had been on a mission, and they were all getting itchy.

"Negative." Jake pulled his ball cap off his head, wiped the sweat from his brow with the back of his wrist, then resettled the hat. The outdoor range on base didn't provide a lot in the way of shade, and it was a warm day in North Carolina. "There's been no word yet on our next vacation destination."

Travis snorted. "We've been sitting on our asses for too damn long. I, for one, want to finish what we started in Sudan."

Jake pinned him with a look. "We don't decide where we go. As far as brass is concerned, that mission is finished."

Ryan toed open an ice chest and handed out bottles of water. "I wouldn't expect anything less. The generals are just politicians with pretty bows and buttons on their chests. After that clusterfuck in Afghanistan—"

"We completed our mission." Jake unscrewed the cap to his water and took a deep swallow. "The politics of it aren't up to us."

"I hate the desert." Chris rolled up unused targets and stuck them in his pack. "I hope our next mission takes us somewhere tropical."

Tony elbowed him. "We won't be drinking daquiris on the beach, dickhead."

Travis chuckled. "It's his hair he's worried about. The dry air fucks with his attempts to style it."

Chris chucked his water bottle at him, and Travis caught it right before it smacked his face.

Jake smothered his grin as he took a swallow of his own water. He'd never had brothers growing up, and he loved the way all the guys on the squad ribbed each other. Their insults ranged from dick size to mental capabilities, and could be as vicious as they were funny. But without a doubt, each man would die for the other.

"Hey, you hear anything more about that chick we pulled from the ocean?" Tony asked.

"Her name is Caroline. Caroline Carter." Jake's humor evaporated. "And she's doing fine. I think."

Travis cocked his head to the side. "You think?"

Jake ground his back teeth together. "She only texted me the once when she got her new phone, saying she had my number. Since then she hasn't responded to me."

The rest of the men hooted. "Psych is being ghosted," Chris said. "And by a woman whose life he saved. It doesn't get more brutal than that."

Jake turned his back on the assholes and placed his weapon in its case. Had he thought he liked the brotherly comradery? Obviously the heat had made him delusional. His men could all go suck it.

"When did you get her number?" Tony hefted his pack over his shoulder.

"At the hospital."

A low whistle sounded behind him. "You went to visit her?" Chris asked.

Jake glared over his shoulder. "Yeah, you got a problem with that?" Fat lot of good it had done him. He'd learned that Caroline would recover physically, but how was she doing mentally? After an experience like that, she must be terrified. And she wouldn't talk to him, let him help her. It was driving him nuts.

Chris held his hands up. "No problem. Just wondering what's different about this chick."

Jake slammed the lid of his rifle case shut. "Aside from the fact that she was almost killed, swam through the dead of night, and found a buoy to cling to, surviving against all odds?"

"She's got guts, I'll give her that." Tony tossed the empty water bottles into the cooler.

"She wasn't bad looking, either." Chris waggled his eyebrows. "Her bra and underwear were more revealing than a bikini."

Jake clenched his fist. "She was nearly drowned, asshole. Have some respect." He hated that the other men had seen her like that. They were all good guys and had ignored her curves when she'd been in danger, just as Jake had. They might joke and make light of situations, but they'd do anything to help a woman.

But Jake still didn't like that they had seen Caroline at her most vulnerable.

When he'd found her on the buoy, he'd thought of nothing but getting her warm and safe. He'd ignored how her body felt in his arms. Ignored the plump mouth and beautiful eyes.

When he'd seen her at the hospital, however, he hadn't been able to ignore her appeal any longer. It had dug under his skin. She was sexy as well as intriguing. He wanted to hear the thoughts that would spill from her lips just as much as he wanted to do filthy things with that mouth.

"All of you need to wipe the image of Caroline in her underwear from your minds. Got it?" He narrowed his eyes and stared at each of his friends. "She's not some random girl you pick up at the bar. She deserves respect."

"They all deserve respect," Tony said. He drew his eyebrows together. "They're just joking around. You know that."

"Don't joke about her."

His men looked at each other and nodded. "No problem, Psych. You're interested in her. No more jokes."

Travis hefted the ice chest onto his shoulder. "Psych has a woman. Never thought I'd see the day."

"She's not mine," Jake growled. But even as he said the words, his body rebelled. It knew. He wanted Caroline to be his. She'd been through a traumatic event, though. Been betrayed by a man she'd been on a date with. He understood why she might be jumpy about answering another guy's text.

He understood, but he didn't like it.

"Hey." Tony jerked his chin at the man in uniform striding toward them down the path. "Boss man's coming."

Their Team Leader, Special Operations Officer Captain Price, stepped in front of them, nodding at each man. The narrow shadow cast from his lanky frame sliced across Jake's face. The creases in his khaki short-sleeve shirt were starting to wilt in the humidity.

Jake straightened. "Good afternoon, sir."

"Gunnery Sergeant Skinner. I'd like a word." The man rubbed the small scar that bisected his lips. "Alone."

Jake bobbed his head at his men. "I'll catch up with you later."

"Drinks at *The Limber Ginger* later?" Chris asked.

Tony blew out a breath. "You know the women I like aren't going to that bar. How about—"

"So, *The Limber Ginger* at seven?" Chris ignored Tony's glare. "You're invited, as well, sir," he threw in as an afterthought.

"Thanks for the offer," Price said dryly. He waited for everyone else to clear out before speaking. "I read your report about the incident on the beach. Good work rescuing that woman."

Jake scraped his palm across his jaw. "I'm just happy as hell we took our swim at that location." He thought about all the ways it could have gone wrong. How Caroline could have been alone at sea for days, all because some douche put profits above poisoning people. "Any word on who this Diaz character is?"

Price lifted his cover, ran his fingers through his tight black curls before replacing it. "The description Ms. Carter gave the police wasn't great, but it could be Julian Diaz, the son of Cristian Diaz, head of the Melledin Cartel. We know there's been a rift between father and son. Diaz, Junior has been trying to build his own empire."

Jake's chest went tight. He prayed Caroline had escaped a different Diaz. Cartel leaders didn't tend to let witnesses live. "Selling to the towns around Camp Lejeune is a bold move. Some of that shit has to be filtering down to the military."

Price inhaled sharply, his nostrils flaring. "And base command isn't happy about it."

"Unhappy enough to let me look into it?" Jake flexed his hand. After what this Diaz had done to Caroline, he wanted to meet him, up close and in person.

"That's not our mission," the SOO said. "You know it's the SEALs who deal in Counter Narcotics. We don't. Besides, it might not even be the right Diaz. There are a lot of Diaz's in the world."

Jake crossed his arms. "Yes, but this Diaz is trespassing in our neighborhood. He's threatened a local woman." The back of his neck went hot. No way was he going to let Caroline get hurt again.

"The police don't think she's in danger," Price said. "I spoke to the chief. He pulled the patrols around her house."

"What?" Jake's shoulders shot back. "They left her alone and unprotected?"

The SOO eyed him. "Is this personal, Skinner?"

"Damn straight." He'd helped many people in his career. Cared about the safety and well-being of each of them. But Caroline was different.

Price sighed. "We can't use government resources to assist a girlfriend. But," he continued before Jake could object, "if you happen to gather information on your own time I wouldn't be upset." His mouth pressed into a flat line. "We had an overdose on base last month, a 19-year-old Marine. I would love to see this asshole go down."

Jake remembered the fear in Caroline's eyes. How desperately she'd clung to him. His gut-wrenching need to get her to safety. Diaz had done that to her. He needed to pay.

One side of his mouth curled. "It would be my absolute pleasure, sir."

Chapter Six

"You've been ignoring me."

Caroline yelped, spinning like a top on her front doorstep, her key scraping the flaking paint on the door.

Jake stood before her, the afternoon sun glinting off his aviator glasses. He was wearing jeans and a t-shirt, every inch of the denim and cotton molding to his muscles.

She shut her mouth with a snap and swallowed. It didn't matter that he looked better than a chocolate cheesecake after a three-mile run. He was off-limits. Even if remembering the feel of his arms around her had been the only thing that had chased away her nightmares the past couple of days. He was military. She'd sworn she'd never go there.

"Ignoring you?" She tittered uncomfortably. "I don't know what you're talking about."

He shoved his sunglasses to the top of his head. With her standing on her front stoop and him on the ground, they were about eye-level.

His gaze bore into her. "Caroline—"

The door squealed behind her, and she jumped again, her purse tumbling to the ground.

"I thought I heard you out here." Sam stood in the doorway. "Hi Jake. Tequila?" she asked Caroline.

Pressing a hand to her heart, Caroline blew out a breath. "If we have any left it will be in the second cupboard to the right of the fridge."

Sam nodded. "I'm making watermelon margaritas, Jake. Hope you can join us." Then she disappeared back inside.

"Are you always this jumpy?" Jake bent and scooped up her purse. He placed a tin of mints and a lip gloss that had spilled from it back inside and handed her the bag.

She took it, careful not to touch him. She didn't need any reminders of how good contact with him felt. "Not usually. I haven't been sleeping well."

That small muscle in his jaw ticked. It seemed to be the only display of anger he let himself show. "It will get better. But after a traumatic event like that, maybe you should talk to someone."

"A shrink?" She snorted. "Too expensive. I'm still waiting to see the bill I'll get for the ambulance ride and hospital stay." Her gut churned. Just when she was starting to get on top of her mom's old medical bills, now she was stuck with her own.

She flushed as Jake examined her house, his eyes scanning the peeling paint, the tarp on her roof that covered the leak she hadn't repaired yet.

"Your job doesn't provide you with insurance?" he asked.

"It does." She hefted her purse higher on her shoulder. "But it doesn't cover everything. Don't worry about it. It will be tight, but I'm doing okay."

She shifted from foot to foot. When he looked at her that way, she felt exposed, like he could see all her secrets.

"You can talk to me anytime," he finally said. "It won't cost you a dime, and I've been in some tight situations, as well."

She raised her chin. "I appreciate all you've done for me, but I don't—"

"No tequila, no watermelon, and no food." Sam poked her head out the door. "Not unless you count that bag of tater tots in the freezer as food, which I do not. We need to go shopping."

Caroline pinched her forehead. The night she'd come home from the hospital they had ordered pizza and wings, and had pretty much been surviving off the leftovers since then. She should have stopped at the store on her way home from work. Plus, if she had she might have missed seeing Jake and all his tempting hotness.

"Okay," she said. "Make a list of what you want to eat. I'll drive."

"Or I could take you two ladies out to dinner." Jake hooked his thumbs in his pockets. "I'd make every man in the restaurant jealous with you two on my arms."

"That's very nice of you," Caroline began.

"Are your marine buddies going to be there?" Sam asked.

Jake scratched his jaw. "They're at *The Limber Ginger*, a bar we like to hang out at. It's only burgers and—"

"Sold." Sam pumped her fist in the air.

"I don't think—" Caroline started.

"I know you don't date military guys, but I am a red-blooded woman who happens to like muscles and bravery." Sam planted her hands on her hips. "Don't take this from me, CeCe."

Caroline sighed. "Fine." A burger and fries did sound good. And she would pay for her and Sam so no one would get the wrong idea.

Sam did a little happy dance before darting back inside. "Give me five minutes," she called, her voice echoing down the hallway.

Jake stepped up next to her. He leaned close. "You don't date military?" His breath gusted across her ear, sending a shiver straight down her spine. He smelled of soap and man, and she inhaled deeply.

"Nope." She shook her head. "Nuh uh. Not ever." Though she struggled to remember why at the moment.

"Hmm." He narrowed his eyes. "That's another conversation we'll be having tonight."

Her pulse fluttered in her throat. "It is?"

"You can count on it."

She looked up into his face. He was much too close. If she rolled onto her toes, she could brush her lips across his mouth. Feel the slight scruff on his jaw. She took a hasty step back. All things she wouldn't be doing.

"Do you want to change?" Jake asked.

Caroline glanced down at her clothes. She was wearing a houndstooth pencil skirt, white blouse, and her black jacket that went with all of her work outfits. It wasn't the sexiest outfit she owned, but it should be fine for burgers and fries.

Especially when she had no interest in attracting this man. "This isn't a date," she warned.

He shrugged. "I just thought you might want to get comfortable instead of wearing professional clothes all day. But suit yourself."

She shifted on her heels, her toes pinching. Well, there was nothing wrong with getting more comfortable. "I'll be just a moment," she said. "Come on in."

Jake followed her into the house, his eyes taking in everything at a glance. The cramped living room lay to the left off the entrance. The kitchen was to the right, its counters cluttered with a near empty tequila bottle, glasses, and a blender that Sam had left out. The bedrooms were at the end of the hall with the bathroom in between.

Caroline pointed to the blue velvet sofa she'd scored at a thrift-store. "I'll be just a minute. You can wait there."

He nodded. He dropped down onto the couch and tossed his arm over the backrest, looking as comfortable as a cat lounging in the sun. Looking for all the world like he belonged in her space.

She hurried to her bedroom. She forced herself not to look in the mirror to check her makeup, because this definitely wasn't a date. In fact, this was so not a date that it didn't matter how atrocious her outfit looked. With a smirk, she kicked off her pumps and dug in her closet for her favorite canvas sneakers. After sprinkling some baby powder in the bottom, because even though this most definitely wasn't a date she didn't want sweaty feet, she tugged them on and stepped back into the hall.

Sam jumped out of the way. A quick-change artist, she had pulled on a denim skirt and tank top in a couple of minutes and painted her eyes a sultry smoky gray. Her friend looked her up and down, her gaze stalling on Caroline's footwear. She dipped her chin and nailed her with a look. "Really? Sneaks with your skirt and blazer?"

"Why not?" Caroline said. "This isn't a date." Besides being comfortable, her outfit made it clearer than glass that she wasn't looking to attract Jake's, or anyone's, attention.

"That should drive the point home." Sam shook her head, then hurried Caroline down the hallway. "We're ready," she called.

Jake stood. The edges of his lips tilted upwards when he saw her feet. "Are those manatees?"

Caroline pointed her toe, admiring the smiling gray images she and her mom had painted on the white shoes when she first bought them. "My favorite animal." And the least sexy shoes she owned.

"Shall we hit it, ladies?" he asked.

"You don't need to ask me twice." Sam was out the door and standing beside his SUV in under two seconds.

Caroline walked to the sidewalk and the passenger door more slowly. Jake opened Caroline's door, and she forced herself to ignore the quiver in her stomach as she brushed past his arm to sit.

She turned to Sam in the back and chatted, catching up on her day as they drove through town.

Jake listened in silence, seemingly unbothered by being ignored.

She ground her teeth. She was trying to send a message, damn it. In big, neon letters that she wasn't interested. But what was the point when he was pretending like he wasn't seeing it?

When they pulled into the parking lot of a rowdy bar and grill she'd been to only a couple times before, she was quick to get out of the car before he could come around to open her door.

"Is this a military hang out?" Sam shielded her eyes from the last rays of the sun.

"One of them," Jake said.

"I'll make a note of that." Sam skipped inside, Jake and Caroline following. They were hit with a blast of upbeat music, cheerful conversations, and a couple of hoots and hollers from the younger guys by the pool tables.

Jake raised his hand to acknowledge a group of men at a round table in the corner of the restaurant. With his hand on Caroline's lower back, he guided them over.

"We didn't think we'd be seeing you tonight," one of the men said. He was obviously military with his short hair and big muscles. They all stood at their approach. "But here Psych shows up not only with one woman, but with two."

Sam looked back at Caroline and mouthed 'wow.'

Caroline swallowed. Being towered over by four tall, ripped, good-looking men was like being in a forest of testosterone. Even with her no-military-men rule, well, it had an impact.

"Gentlemen." Jake nodded at the men as he pulled some chairs from nearby tables. "I tried to tell these two the company here would be lousy, but—"

One of the men, with blond hair and sparkling blue eyes, elbowed Jake out of his way and stuck out his hand to Sam. "Ryan Kelly, at your service, ma'am."

Jake rubbed his ribs and made the introductions. Aside from Ryan, there was Anthony Garcia, a naval officer with dark hair and eyes and shoulders that seemed impossibly wide, and Travis Kowalski, with reddish-brown hair and an impish smile. All the men were tall and well-built, but Caroline couldn't help but notice that Jake's body was the sexiest. His muscles were thick and solid, and his chest was just the right height to rest her cheek against if they were standing close.

"Where's Chris?" Jake asked.

"Already found a lady friend for the night and taken off." Tony frowned, looking slightly disapproving.

Sam checked the time on her phone. "It's not even seven thirty. He works fast."

"He does everything fast. Everything," Ryan said, heavy with innuendo. He smirked. "Let's not waste time talking about him. How about you and I get to know each other better?" He pulled out a chair next to his and made a sweeping hand gesture toward it.

Sam rolled her eyes and sat next to Tony instead. "Jake said you were an officer in the Navy? I thought you were all Marines?"

"Every Raider squad has one Special Amphibious Reconnaissance Corpsman from the Navy embedded in it. That's me." Tony arched an eyebrow. "The jarheads discovered they couldn't get by without us."

A rousing chorus of jeers followed that statement. Tony dodged a balled-up paper napkin.

"You know Psych is going to make you pay for that next training session." Travis's face lit with glee. "I'm going to bring popcorn."

"Psych?" Caroline asked.

"My nickname." Jake helped her scoot her chair in then sat beside her. "I've had some good hunches over the years. The name stuck."

"It's good to see you looking so well, Caroline," Tony said. "Last time we met, you were more ice cube than human."

She flushed. "I know all of you helped rescue me. I can't tell you how much I appreciate it. Thank you."

"Rescuing beautiful women is all in a day's work." Ryan winked, then waved over a waitress. They put in an order for more food and drink.

Sam planted her elbows on the table on Caroline's other side. She glanced around the bar. "Why is it called *The Limber Ginger*?"

"No one knows." Ryan propped his ankle over his knee. "And we've asked. The owner, Kieran, is definitely a ginger, but I don't even want to imagine him bending that body." He gave a faux shiver. "But their prices are fair, and they put up with raising hell late into the night, so we like it."

Sam craned her head and pointed at the small dance floor near the back. "Does anyone actually dance?"

"Usually when it gets a little later and people get drunker," Ryan said.

"But someone has to start things off." Travis stood and held out a hand to Sam. "Shall we?" And with a smirk at Ryan, he tugged Sam to her feet and led her to the parquet floor.

Tony hooted. "He snagged her out from under you."

Ryan grumbled good-naturedly. He looked toward Caroline. "I don't suppose...."

Jake laid his arm on the seat back behind Caroline's shoulders.

Ryan sighed. "No, I guess not."

Caroline tapped her toe at the next song that came on. It had been a while since she'd been out with anyone but Sam. Even though she only knew Jake, she was comfortable with his friends. She started to relax until Jake leaned in close.

"How about it?" he said. "Shall we join our friends on the dance floor?"

Caroline flushed. "I'm not much of a dancer." She loved dancing. But dancing led to touching. Touching led to relationships. And that was something that couldn't happen.

"Come on," he cajoled. He stood and pulled her to her feet. "You've got your dancing shoes on and everything." He jerked his chin at her feet.

She chewed on her bottom lip. Her manatees did like to kick up their heels. Besides, one dance couldn't hurt. "As friends," she said.

"For now," he agreed. He took her arm and led her to the floor. Sam was shaking her stuff, laughing at something Travis had said. Caroline rolled her shoulders. They were just two women out for a good time.

That assurance lasted all of ten seconds. Lasted until Jake pulled her into his arms. He set his own slower pace, ignoring the fast beat of the music. Unwillingly, her body melted against his.

She'd been right. His chest was the perfect height to rest her cheek against.

He clasped her right hand tightly, stroking her skin with his thumb. His other hand was wrapped around her waist. He didn't pull her into his body, but then, he didn't need to. Her body seemed eager to attach itself to his, regardless.

"I'm not going to date you." It was a reminder as much for herself as for Jake.

"Because you don't date military."

She nodded.

"Why is that?"

Her stomach clenched. "I don't want to talk about it."

"All right," he said easily enough, but there was a hard edge to his voice. "Let's talk about you. How are you doing?"

"I'm fine."

He slid his hand up her back and tugged on her ponytail, tipping her head up to face him. "I don't want platitudes. You went through something unimaginable. So tell me again. How are you?" His eyes searched hers. The concern in them was almost her undoing.

She swallowed against the burn in the back of her throat. "I haven't been sleeping well," she admitted. "I keep dreaming about being alone in the ocean, with all that water below me. In my dreams, there's always something deep down, waiting to come up and swallow me whole."

He tucked a strand of hair behind her ear. "You're safe now."

"I know." She looked over his shoulder, then back into his face. There was something about his gaze that did make her feel safe. "But it's not just about that night. I guess I've been feeling pretty adrift in life, as well. My mom is gone now. I'm stuck in a job I don't like. I just feel like I should be doing something else, something more, you know?"

"Then get after it." Jake took her in a slow spin. "You're a fighter. If you want to change your life, you can."

He made it sound so simple. So achievable. And maybe part of it was. When her mom was sick, she'd left college and taken whatever job would pay the bills. With her mom gone, well, she still had bills. But she could explore her options. Start putting out resumes. Maybe even look into night or online courses if she wanted to get her degree. It wouldn't be easy, but after surviving a night with a crazy drug dealer and then a swim in the ocean, she was feeling more confident about her abilities to face a challenge.

She met his beautiful green eyes, got caught in them. "I will," she said. "Thank you." She didn't know when, but at some point their feet had stopped moving. They were in the shadows along the wall. The music had faded in her ears. It felt like they were cocooned in their own private bubble.

Jake slid his hand over her shoulder, along her neck, and cupped her cheek. He lowered his head, and Caroline closed her eyes.

Her heart pounded in her chest. His hand felt like heaven on her skin, and she could only imagine what it would be like if he really touched her. If only—

His lips brushed hers, the kiss gentle, searching.

She sighed into it, and he took it deeper. Jake gripped her waist like he never wanted to let go. The world disappeared around her...until Travis and Sam drew up next to them, wearing identical smirks.

"You're making some of the young bucks jealous, Psych. Unless you want to give tutorials on how to please a lady, you might want to take this somewhere more private."

Sam slapped Travis's arm. "My friend doesn't have nearly enough fun. If she wants to make-out—"

Caroline's stomach clenched. She pulled from Jake's arms and fled. The back of her neck and cheeks burned. Not only had she made a fool of herself in public, but with a man she could never have.

"Caroline, wait." Jake jogged after her. "I'm sorry. I shouldn't have—"

She snagged her purse off the back of her chair without breaking her stride and headed for the exit. "Can you make sure Sam gets home all right?"

"Or course." He grabbed her elbow and pulled her to a stop. "But we need to talk."

"There's nothing to talk about." A fine tremor shook her hands, and she clenched them to her sides. "I know better."

"Better than what?" His eyes searched hers. "Better than to have feelings for a Marine?"

"Feelings?" She huffed out a harsh chuckle. She jerked her chin at the dance floor. "Is that what you think happened back there? It was lust, pure and simple." Her stomach twisted at the words.

His face darkened. "What's going on between us isn't just lust. Don't lie to me or yourself."

She glanced at the doors. They were only feet away, her escape tantalizingly close. "I don't know how many times I have to say it, but I don't—"

"Date military," he finished for her. He crossed his arms over his chest. "Why?"

"My dad was Navy, okay?" The words spilled out, almost clogging her throat. "He was a good-time sailor, and it wasn't long before he realized that having a wife and kid were more responsibility than he wanted. He was military, and he left."

"That's BS." Jake's nostrils flared. "One man's mistakes shouldn't poison your view of every serviceman."

She swallowed. "People who join the military want the adventure. They don't want to be tied down."

He stepped close, the toe of his boot kissing her manatees. "Real men don't leave. I'm sorry you had a father who didn't understand that, but I'm not him. I would never abandon my family."

She stared down at their feet. His was nearly twice the size of hers and looked ready to kick a hole in any argument she made. She blinked at the burn in her eyes. "A couple of years after he left, we were contacted by the Navy. There had been a training accident. He died." She brushed her cheek with the back of her hand and finally met his eyes. "There are lots of ways a military man can leave. You might not like it, but the fact is you have a dangerous job." Especially as a member of the special forces.

He reached for her, but she stepped back. "Did you know I work for an actuarial company? One benefit to working there is that I've become very good at calculating the odds. I won't risk going through what my mom did. I'm sorry, Jake."

She turned on her heel and pushed through the doors, never looking back.

Chapter Seven

JAKE DUCKED UNDER TONY'S right hook. The leg sweep he didn't see until it was too late.

Tony stared down at him, his chest rising and falling with exertion. "What's wrong? Your age finally slowing you down?"

Jake grunted and pushed off the mat. He was maybe two years older than Tony, hardly a disadvantage. He rolled his neck. But the lack of sleep and stiff body from sitting in a car all night had put him off his game.

Travis dropped down from the pull-up bar. He pulled his towel from the bar and wiped his forehead. "Maybe he's wiped from all the running he's been doing. Chasing after a girl who isn't interested must get tiring."

The other guys hooted with laughter.

Jake cracked his knuckles. The problem with the gym on base was that the guys got too chatty. It turned as gossipy as a fucking quilting circle. "She's interested." And scared. He needed to figure out a way to show her he was a safe bet.

"She looked like she was into Psych when his tongue was down her throat, that's for sure." Tony peeled off his grappling gloves. "But the way she hauled ass out of *The Ginger*...."

Ryan pursed his lips. "I haven't seen a woman move that fast since Chris told that pretty little number his philosophy on families."

Jake's lips twitched. That poor schoolteacher hadn't known what she was getting into when she'd asked Chris if he wanted kids someday. All of his men were still in their sowing-oats phase, but Chris seemed to have a particular aversion to starting a family.

His humor drained away. He hadn't thought he was ready to give up the single life either, but he'd damn sure like a chance for a date with Caroline. Explore what was between them.

He didn't know what it was about her. She was pretty but not overtly sexy. But damn, thoughts of her wrapped around him made him hard in an instant.

Jake tossed his gloves in his bag. "She says she won't date military men. Her dad was Navy and he left her as a kid. She's shutting us down before we can even begin."

Ryan's face darkened. "Having a parent leave you can be a real mind-fuck. Tread lightly."

Chris handed Ryan a bottle of water then slapped him on the back. They all knew Ryan's mom had disappeared on him and his dad when he was a teenager. Some wounds healed slower than others.

"I'm not her father," Jake growled.

"No, but add to that the fact that she's going through all this shit now, that she might have a cartel leader after her, and it's no wonder she's jumpy. She probably just needs some space." Tony hefted his bag to his shoulder, and they headed to the showers.

"Ooh, did you learn all that from watching Oprah?" Travis asked.

"Dr. Phil, asshole." Tony shrugged. "How's Caroline doing anyway?"

Jake pushed through the doors, a wave of steam slamming into him. "She doesn't know her Diaz might be Julian Diaz. I didn't tell her."

Chris paused, his shirt halfway over his head. "You didn't tell her she might have a cartel after her? Why the hell not?"

"What would she do with that information? She has enough to deal with as it is." Jake shoved his bag into his locker and kicked off his shoes.

His friends gave each other looks, ones Jake didn't especially care for. "What?" he barked.

"I understand you wanting her to feel safe," Tony said, "but this could be useful information to her. If it really is Cristian Diaz's son she met, she's a sitting duck."

"And she has Sam staying with her." Ryan frowned. "That woman is feisty, but I don't think she'll be much protection."

"Who's Sam?" Chris asked.

"Caroline's friend," Jake said.

"Caroline's sexy friend," Ryan amended.

Jake glared at him. "And I didn't leave her without protection." His temperature spiked. He couldn't believe his friends would think he could do that. "I have a buddy of mine watching her to and from work. He's retired police."

"And you're watching when she's home." Tony smirked. "My easy beat-down of you today makes more sense."

"You had one lucky kick." Jake ran his hand up the back of his head. "But yeah, I followed her in the cab she took home from the bar and stayed the night in my vehicle across the street."

"Which is why you had me drive Sam home." Travis nodded in understanding.

"How hot is this Sam?" Chris wrapped a towel around his waist.

"Smokin'." Travis laughed. "She's also way too smart to get involved with commitment-phobes like you or Ryan."

"But—"

"Can you stop thinking with your dick for five minutes?" Jake slammed his locker shut. "Sam isn't the issue here. Caroline's safety is."

Their faces sobered. "Sorry, Psych," Travis said. "You know we'll do anything we can to help. What do we know?"

Jake exhaled slowly. None of this was his men's fault. He shouldn't snap at them just because they weren't wound as tightly as he was over the situation. "This buddy of mine still has contacts in the force." Jake flexed his hand. "He says that no boat matching Caroline's description was berthed in the harbor that day."

Three guys from another squad tossed them a greeting as they passed. Tony waited until they were gone. "He paid off the harbor master to stay off the books?"

"Looks like." Jake slung his towel around the back of his neck and gripped the ends. "I've got a bad feeling about all of this. I need to find this Diaz, and fast." He and his men could be sent on a mission at an hour's notice. He'd never minded it before, but the thought of leaving Caroline here, alone and unprotected, when someone might be after her....

His jaw ached with how hard he clenched it. He had to find this asshole. Anything else was unacceptable.

Ryan grabbed a bottle of shampoo from his locker. "I've been needing to hone my computer skills. I'll see what I can find out about this guy from government sources."

"Is that a euphemism for hacking into the systems of three-letter agencies?" Travis arched an eyebrow.

Ryan shrugged. "Like I said, I need some practice."

Chris nodded. "And the rest of us have time for a little protection detail. If you don't want her to know we're there, she'll never see us."

The muscles in Jake's back released. He should have come to his men earlier with his worries. If they made it their mission to keep Caroline safe, she would be.

His other problem the guys couldn't help him with, but he wasn't going to give up on it, either. He and Caroline had a connection, one he'd never felt so strongly with another woman. He only had to convince Caroline to act on it.

"She'll be getting home from work soon. I'll head over there and relieve my friend." Jake headed for the showers. "I'll let you guys know if I need you." If everything went as planned, he wouldn't. He might not be able to persuade Caroline to give him a chance, not yet, but he would damn sure get her to accept his help.

Her life might depend upon it.

Chapter Eight

CAROLINE YANKED A CLUMP of prickly purple flowers from her front lawn. They were pretty, but they didn't belong there. A feeling that was becoming much too familiar.

A gray SUV cruised down the street. Caroline clenched a set of small clippers, her body tensing, until she saw Jake's face behind the steering wheel.

He pulled to the curb in front of her house and stepped out. "Caroline." His gaze flicked to her bare legs then back to her face.

She pushed up to standing. All she could see of him was his face and shoulders, but damn, what a face, what shoulders. Everything about this man was drool-worthy.

Everything except his job.

Her unwanted attraction to him made her voice come out sounding more petulant than she would have liked. "What are you doing here?" She'd told him she wasn't interested, and even if it was a lie, he had no right coming around in his faded blue t-shirt with his dark hair slightly damp and curling. He looked good enough to eat.

He'd probably come right from a shower, and her mind automatically pictured just how magnificent Jake, naked, soaping himself clean, in a shower would look.

She scraped her teeth across her lower lip. Did he run a bar of soap along the edges of all those muscles or did he—

"We have to talk." Jake rounded his car and joined her on the lawn. "I have a picture I'd like to show you. Tell me if it's Diaz."

A crescendo of wails rose from inside her house, and Caroline closed her eyes, her shoulders drooping. She was so tired. Of being afraid. Of the unholy noises her best friend created. Of fighting her attraction to Jake.... She needed a weekend away to get her head sorted.

"What's that?" Jake grimaced.

"Sam is playing some zombie video game. I think it's turned into an addiction." And after playing until two that morning, somehow Sam had looked as perky as the Energizer Bunny heading off to work while Caroline's feet had dragged.

She loved Sam, but having her as a roomie sucked.

"Ah." Jake strode for her front door.

Caroline trotted after him. "What are you doing?"

"Fixing your problem." He stepped into her house and turned to the living room. Sam hadn't turned on the lights, and the TV flashed eerily through the evening dusk. "Hi, Sam."

Her friend held up a finger before working her controller furiously. Something exploded on the screen, and she pumped her hand in the air. "Yes!" She tossed the controller aside. "Hey, what's up?"

"You're relieved of duty." Jake cocked his shoulder against the wall. "I'll make sure Caroline is safe tonight."

Caroline's mouth dropped open. Of all the nerve, thinking he could manage who would or wouldn't be staying at her house. Thankfully, she had a friend who was as loyal and stubborn as—

"Great." Sam hopped up. "I'd love to sleep in my own bed again. No offense, but the mattress in your guest bedroom is a little...." She rocked her hand side to side.

Caroline narrowed her eyes. "Traitor." And she didn't mean the comment about the mattress.

Sam stepped close and gave her a hug. "He's not your dad, CeCe," she whispered. "Give him a chance."

Jake watched Sam bound down the hall to get her stuff and straightened. "I don't mind a lumpy mattress, but I'm also happy to crash on your couch. Hell, I'll even stay in my SUV again if that's what you're comfortable with. But you can sleep easy. I'll keep you safe."

She shook her head. "Wait. Stay in your SUV? Again?"

He nodded.

"You've been sleeping outside my house?" She shuffled back a step.

He nodded again.

"I, uh, thanks." Her face went warm. That was...sweet. Or maybe stalkerish? She cocked her head, examining him. Everything about Jake Skinner screamed dependability. From his solid muscles that looked like he could carry any burden to the concerned expression on his face. He was worried. About her. And had slept outside in a car to watch over her.

Definitely sweet.

She rubbed at a bit of dirt on her wrist, avoiding his gaze. She didn't quite know what to do with this man. She knew what her body wanted to do with him, but her brain, and heart, knew that was out of the question. "You had a picture you wanted me to look at?"

He was silent a beat. "Right." He pulled a folded photo from his pocket and handed it to her. "Was this the man on the yacht?"

The picture was grainy, the man's features indistinct. He was looking off to the side, not directly at the camera. She thought back to that night, tried to match her memory of the man's nose, his jaw, to the photo.

"I don't know." She stepped across to the kitchen, flipping on the lights, and examined the picture again. She waved a goodbye to Sam as she hollered from the front door, but she didn't take her eyes from the photograph. "It could be him. Is this the best picture you have?"

Jake sighed. "Unfortunately. He's done a good job of keeping off the radar. And the focus has always been on his father."

"Who is it?"

He took the photo back and slid it into his back pocket. "The man in the picture is Julian Diaz, the son of Cristian Diaz. The father is the head of the Melledin Cartel. His son might be trying to make a name for himself, expanding into US territory."

Caroline felt behind her for the counter and sagged against it. "A cartel leader?" The contents of her stomach swirled uneasily. Being shot at by cartel leaders didn't happen to normal people. It was like her life had turned into a crime drama. "And you think he's looking for me."

Jake squeezed her shoulder. "There's no evidence of that."

He sounded like her mom's doctors when they were trying to soft-pedal the bad diagnoses. And the man had slept in his car to watch her house. He must think Diaz was looking for her. "But?"

"But I'm going to make sure you stay safe."

Her muscles loosened. Jake sounded absolutely confident and one hundred percent determined. She believed him.

Still.... "You know you don't have to. I'm not your responsibility." Her heart thumped. She needed to give him the out, and a part of her hoped he'd take it. But the sensible side of her, the one who feared a broken neck over a broken heart, wanted to slap herself upside the head for even suggesting it.

His jade gaze pierced her. "I don't think we've determined quite what you are to me, but you're definitely something."

She swallowed. "But the police—"

"Have pulled their patrols." He shook his head. "There's no protection from that quarter."

"So you're all I've got?"

"Is that so bad?"

She focused on his lips. His eyes were too intense. They seemed to see right into the heart of her. "No," she finally said. "No, it's not."

He slid his hand down her arm, sending up sparks wherever he touched, before stepping back. "Are you hungry? I need to eat."

Caroline winced. "I still haven't gone shopping."

"No problem, we can go out."

She rolled the hem of her tank top between her fingers. Her pulse fluttered in her throat. "Go out?" She went out all the time, but now that a cartel member was potentially looking for her.... "Why don't we go grocery shopping and stay in? Where we won't be a target."

"Sweetheart." Jake tucked a strand of hair behind her ear, and she instinctively leaned into his touch. "You'll be safe wherever we go, I promise, but I do have an idea for somewhere you should feel completely comfortable." One edge of his lips quirked up. "Trust me?"

She didn't want to. Trust was the foundation for a relationship, and she was not getting into a relationship with this man. Probably. She needed to dig deep for some will-power.

She sighed. "Yes. I trust you."

He grinned. "Perfect. Now, do you have a blanket you don't mind getting dirty?"

The sky was a swirl of purples and grays over the Atlantic. Jake crumpled the wax wrapper of his sandwich and sat back on his hands, the plaid blanket a thin barrier to the sand below. Caroline sat cross-legged beside him, ensconced in the sweatshirt he kept in his vehicle.

"You have a little mustard..." Jake wiped a smudge beneath her lower lip. "Right there."

Caroline flushed. "Thanks." She shoved her garbage into a plastic bag then drew her knees to her chest, wrapping her arms around them.

"You still cold?" The evening air felt good on his bare arms, but he didn't like the little shiver that went through her body.

"No, it's just...." She looked at her bare feet, peeping out from beneath his sweatshirt. Her toenails were painted a pretty shade of pink. "I appreciate you taking me to this beach on base. Knowing strangers can't just walk in here does make me feel more secure."

"But?"

She rested her cheek on her knees. "You're going to think I'm an idiot."

"I don't think that's possible." And it wasn't. The more time he spent with her, the more time he wanted. Caroline was the perfect mix of sassy, sweet, and stubborn. Although, when the stubborn was turned his way, it wasn't his favorite personality trait.

She nibbled on her bottom lip. "I used to love the ocean. I spent almost all my weekends at the beach growing up. But after that night—" She pressed her lips tight.

"You're scared to go back in the water." Swimming in deep water, especially in the dark, could be a mind-fuck. Jake had known Marines who'd had panic attacks while training in the ocean. He could only imagine the terror Caroline had felt swimming all alone with thousands of feet of water beneath her.

"Even looking at the ocean brings back memories of that night. I can't imagine ever swimming in it again." She brushed sand off the blanket. "You probably think I'm a coward. You're some special forces Rambo; you probably laugh when you jump from a plane."

"That's the last thing I think." He rested his hand on her hunched shoulder. "Caroline, look at me."

She flicked her fingers beneath her eye but kept her face toward the sea.

Jake frowned. He cupped her chin and turned her head. "Even special forces feel fear. No one can avoid it. We train to work through it, however." He rubbed his thumb along her velvety-soft cheek. Her eyes glimmered with the last rays of the day's light.

"I guess I could use a little bit of that training, huh?" She laughed weakly.

Jake's heart clenched. She was so strong, and she didn't even realize it. He rolled to his feet and held out his hand. "Come on. Let's try something."

Warily, she slid her palm over his, and he pulled her to standing. "We're not going to go skydiving, are we? I don't think I could handle your kind of training."

"Nope." He pulled his shirt over his head then smiled wickedly. "But we're going to get a little wet."

He kicked out of his trousers until all he wore were his boxer shorts.

"Exposure therapy?" Caroline scraped her teeth over her bottom lip, her eyes flicking to his chest, his thighs, then back to his face.

He thought her cheeks might have turned pink, but in the twilight, it was impossible to tell. He loved the idea that he could make her blush.

"Why not?" He took her hand again and waggled his eyebrows. "Just call me Dr. Skinner."

Her chuckle this time was sincere. "Okay, *doctor*. But all I promise is to dip my toes in the water."

He went half-hard at the throaty way she called him 'doctor,' and all sorts of fun role-plays ran through his mind. Her playing nurse. Her playing patient. He bit back a groan.

For another time. Tonight was about Caroline. "Your toes are a good start."

They strolled down to the surf. Low waves lapped onto the shore, and moonlight glinted off the water. Caroline hesitated at the waterline, her hand tightening around his.

Jake stepped in to his ankles. "The water feels great tonight. It's nice and wa-aargh!" He hopped up and down, shaking his foot.

"What is it?!" Caroline reached for him. "Oh my God, is it a jellyfish?"

Jake gave one last moan, before hunching over laughing.

Caroline gaped at him. "You jerk." She slapped his arm. "Don't do that to me."

He grabbed her wrist as she swiped at him again and tugged her close. "Sorry, but you should have seen your face." His chuckles tapered off. "Besides, look where you're standing now."

She looked at where the water swirled around her knees. "I'm in the ocean."

"That you are." He placed his hands at her hips. "How do you feel?"

"Still mad at you." She pursed her lips. "But not scared."

"How about a little deeper?" Jake stepped back, the water going to his thighs. "We could go for a swim."

Caroline inhaled sharply. "I don't think I'm ready for that, but maybe just a couple steps farther." She hooked her thumbs in the waistband of her shorts and shimmied them down her legs.

His mouth went as dry as an uncooked MRE. "What are you doing?" The bottom of her shorts dragged in the water before she slipped her legs free. She tossed the shorts back onto the sand. Her bare thighs were but shapely shadows, but his memory filled in what his vision couldn't.

"I don't want to sit in wet shorts on the ride home." Caroline rolled up the sleeves of the sweatshirt and tugged up the hem. "But my top is staying on. I won't be going deep enough to get it wet," she warned.

"Whatever you feel comfortable with." Jake's chest swelled with pride as she took one slow step forward, then another. Water rose to the shadowed valley between her thighs, and he bit back a groan.

Caroline's hand started to tremble. "Jake?"

"Right here." He stepped close and wrapped his arms around her waist. He kissed the top of her head. "You're doing great, sweetheart."

A bitter chuckle burst from her lips. "I'm only hip-deep in the ocean and I'm petrified." Her chest scraped against his with its rapid rise and fall. "I can't see what might be there. What might swim up and—"

"Shh." He slipped his hand under her sweatshirt and tank top and rubbed her lower back. Her skin was clammy against his palm. "You don't have to do a night swim your first time back in the water. You're out here, facing your fear. You're doing amazingly."

She tucked her head against his chest, and he couldn't ignore how right it felt, Caroline curled up against him. Waves gently lapped against their bodies, and moonlight cast a long tail over the ocean's surface.

"It's not so bad with you holding me," she murmured.

"Yeah?"

Caroline tilted her head up. Her breath caressed his jaw. "I'm sorry I've been so horrible to you. I just can't let myself...."

"You have nothing to apologize for." He kneaded her lower back. "But fair warning, the motto of the Marines is to Improvise, Adapt, and Overcome. I'm going to keep working on those walls of yours. And I'm going to succeed in knocking them down."

She pressed her forehead against his skin. "Jake, I—"

"Right now, what are you feeling?" He didn't want to hear her saying they couldn't be together again. Not tonight. "Don't worry about the future, or what we will or won't be. This moment, right now, what do you want?"

She blinked. "I want...."

"Yes?"

She sighed, long and low. "I want this." Gripping him behind the neck, she pulled herself up an inch and pressed her lips to his.

Electricity shot down his spine. Her mouth was soft, exploring, and she tasted faintly of salt. It was the sweetest, most sensuous kiss of his life, and they'd only just touched. The fact that she allowed herself to do this at all absolutely floored him.

She pulled back and sucked in a deep breath. "Oh, my. That was...."

"Fucking amazing." Jake cupped the back of her head and reeled her back in. He took advantage of her moan, sweeping his tongue inside her mouth, tasting every inch of her. Her soft curves molded to his hard body. He cursed the lack of a bed, a beach, anywhere he could lay her out and bare every delicious bit of her.

Caroline hooked her leg around his hip, rocking into him with each thrust of her tongue.

His cock ached, the heat of her core achingly close, only separated by the thin layer of her panties and his boxers.

"Let me make you feel good." Jake slid his palm inside her underwear and cupped one plump cheek. He held her steady as he rubbed his erection against her slit. Every muscle in his body tensed. He longed to slide into her heat, take her hard and fast, show her just how good they could be together.

But more than that, he wanted to build the foundation to something lasting, and rushing Caroline into something she might regret later wasn't the way to get there. He needed to make this solely about her, and hopefully, change her memories of the ocean from fear to something that would make her smile.

"Yes." Her voice was low, breathy. Her nails dug into the back of his neck, and he welcomed the small bite of pain. It helped him keep control.

He slid his hand further down her panties, finding her lower lips slick with her desire. He traced the edges of her labia, circled her opening until her breath caught, stalled.

"Don't tease," she said.

His lips curved against her temple. Teasing Caroline was going to become one of his favorite hobbies, he could tell. But he didn't think she'd appreciate that information just yet.

She angled her hips, increasing the friction between them, and Jake eased his finger inside her channel. He ground his jaw. She was hot, wet, and tight, and he almost came right then and there.

He fucked her slowly, adding another finger, taking his cues from every hitch in her breath. He memorized the way she dug her teeth into her lower lip, how the tension in her muscles built. And when her eyes flared wide and latched onto his, Jake circled her clit with his middle finger and watched her explode.

Caroline dug her teeth into his shoulder, muffling her whimpers. He toyed with her tender flesh until she went limp in his arms, her contented sigh the best fucking sound in the world.

"Jake." Her voice was soft, drowsy, and laced with a hint of anxiety. He knew her mind was probably racing, wondering just how this played into her rules about military men.

"I know, sweetheart." He brushed his lips against her forehead. The war for her heart was far from over, but he was counting this battle as one of his wins. One of their wins. "Before you throw those walls up again, I'm going to get you home while I'm still ahead."

"Home." She was quiet a moment. "And you're going to stay there with me?"

"On your couch." For now. When she invited him into her bed, he didn't want there to be any hesitation. No regrets. "It will be the best location for me to hear if anyone tries to get in. Not that I'm expecting that to happen," he was quick to add.

She nodded, then pulled from his arms and turned for the shore. "And just like that reality intrudes."

He followed, placing his hand on her hip, needing the contact, no matter how small.

Improvise. Adapt. Overcome. He'd never thought of those words in relation to a woman before, but the motto was just as important in regards to Caroline as it was to any mission.

"Reality," he said, "is what we make of it."

Chapter Nine

CAROLINE REFORMATTED THE SPREADSHEET according to her boss's latest demands and emailed it over to him. She'd never thought she'd be a person who worked with numbers all day. It was a long way from the English degree she'd been working on before dropping out of college to take care of her mom. She never regretted that decision, but sometimes she wondered, what if? What job would she have now if she had earned her diploma?

One good thing about being an admin for an actuarial firm was that focusing on columns and rows was a sure-fire way of helping her ignore what had happened last night with Jake.

Of the way he'd helped her overcome her fears.

The way he'd held her.

The way he'd make her explode like—

Rats. She was thinking about it again. About him.

Her cheeks heated, and she darted a glance at the other cubicles, certain her co-workers would be able to see the guilt on her face. She couldn't believe she'd let him do that to her, in public no less. It had been a dark and deserted beach, sure, but *someone* might have come along.

She'd dropped her defenses and...it hadn't sucked. Nothing tragic had befallen her. In fact, it had been wonderful. Maybe, *maybe*, she was being just a little bit stubborn about this whole not-dating-military-guys thing.

Maybe.

There were lots of happy marriages in the military, after all. Not that she was thinking about marrying Jake, but she had to admit not all servicemen were like her father.

So why was it so hard to give this one a chance?

Her cell phone rang, and she pulled it out of her desk drawer. An unfamiliar number lit the screen.

She answered it hesitantly. If it was someone calling about a damn car warranty....

"Hello?"

"Ms. Carter? This is Sergeant Schaefer with the Jacksonville Police Department. I was hoping you could come down to the station today and look at a picture for us."

She muffled a groan. More pictures, but maybe the police had a better photo of this Diaz character than Jake had. "All right. My lunch break is in fifteen minutes. I can come down then if that works for you."

He agreed and gave her the station's address.

It was only a ten-minute walk, and after finishing up her work, she grabbed her purse and headed out.

She turned her phone over in her palm as she went down the sidewalk. Should she call Jake? She had a feeling he'd want her to. He'd followed her to work this morning and was coming by this evening to escort her home. She couldn't decide if it felt like he was crowding her or caring for her. Maybe a bit of both.

What Jake Skinner wanted wasn't necessarily what was best. They'd had one hot night but made no promises to each other. And even though she was *maybe* rethinking dating him, she didn't want to become dependent on the man.

She shoved her phone into her purse and picked up her pace. Luckily, she was wearing flats and it was a beautiful day, sunny but not too warm. A hint of the sea was in the air. The sun and the breeze were usually relaxing, but she was going to a police station to identify the man who tried to kill her. Her back remained rigid. The skin between her shoulder blades itched.

She looked behind her, left and right. There was nothing out of the ordinary, just the normal lunch crowd clogging the street and sidewalks. The outdoor café tables were already starting to fill, and cheerful conversations filled the air.

Caroline's anxiety rose. She quickened her pace, the feeling of being watched growing. She only relaxed when she entered the security of the police station.

She smiled at the uniformed cop at the front desk and explained why she was there.

It was only a minute until Sergeant Shaefer came out and guided her back to his office. "Thanks for coming. Ms. Carter. I appreciate you making the trip so quickly."

She settled her purse in her lap. "Do you have a picture of Diaz for me to look at? I heard he might be the son of a cartel leader."

The sergeant ran his fingers through his thinning hair, shooting her a skeptical look. "Diaz is a very common surname. Unfortunately, drug dealers are just as common. The chances that the man on your boat is related to some high-up drug lord are very unlikely."

The back of her neck prickled with embarrassment. Even if her Diaz wasn't *the* Diaz, that didn't give the sergeant the right to look at her like she was an idiot. She wasn't some hysteric. Besides, she'd put stock in Jake's information over the local PD's any day of the week.

Shaefer picked a manila folder up from his desk. "The picture I'm going to show you is disturbing," he said. "It's of a person with a bullet wound in his head. A local fishermen pulled the body from the ocean early this morning. Can you tell me if you recognize this man?" He opened the folder and placed it before her on the desk.

Caroline sucked in a breath, steeling herself before lowering her gaze to the photo. Her lungs stalled. "It's Brent." She felt the spray of his brain matter hitting her face all over again. Of seeing a hole appear where one should never be. The back of her throat ached. The coroner had done a good job repairing the exit wound, but it was still a shock seeing his dead body.

"Are you sure it's him?" Shaefer pressed.

She looked back at the picture, trying to avoid the wound on his temple, the pallor of his skin.

The bloat.

She swallowed. "Yes, it's the man who took me to that yacht."

The sergeant closed the folder. "Thank you. I want you to go over that night again. Tell me every detail you can remember."

She sagged back in the chair and repeated her story. She was having a hard time dredging up any sympathy for Brent. Although she didn't think he had the balls to personally pull the trigger on her, he'd gotten her into this mess.

A mess that had resulted in her meeting Jake. She blew out a breath. She didn't like the idea that she should feel gratitude to Brent for anything.

Shaefer held out his hand to shake. "We'll be in touch. There's every chance your Diaz killed this man and then moved on. He'd have to be stupid to stick around, but we'll keep an eye out."

"And the patrols around my house?" she asked.

He rubbed the back of his neck. "I'm afraid we didn't have the resources to maintain those."

How many resources did it take to have a patrol car drive by her house once an hour? But she only said, "Of course." She wasn't the type to raise a fuss, something she was starting to regret.

She thought about asking if they at least had the resources to give her a ride back to work. The memory of feeling like someone had followed her lingered, but she thought better of getting snarky with the police. And any ride Sergeant Shaefer might give her would be accompanied by pity for the poor, panicked, delusional woman who thought a cartel might be after her.

It was broad daylight and she was in the middle of town. She hefted her purse on her shoulder. She would be fine.

Caroline nodded goodbye and strode from the building. She kept her head down, her gaze darting furiously left and right. She never saw anyone suspicious when she looked over her shoulder, but she felt someone there, watching.

Maybe she *was* paranoid. Maybe Sergeant Shaefer was right to pity her. She'd changed that night in the ocean, become someone less trusting and more prone to see threats wherever she went. She didn't know if she'd ever get back to a life without fear.

Horns blared in the intersection ahead. A blue sedan smashed into the side of a Jeep going the other way. Traffic clogged as both drivers got out to look over the damage. Bystanders blocked the sidewalk, one of them pulling out his phone to record the incident as the drivers' voices became heated.

Instead of fighting through the crowd, Caroline turned down a side street to circle around the mess. The heels of her flats slapped against the pavement as the street grew quieter.

She turned left at the next intersection. A plastic bag tumbled across the empty street, and the feeling between her shoulder blades grew from an itch to an inferno of fire ants crisscrossing her skin.

Her breathing sped up. She was an idiot. She never should have left the main street.

She glanced over her shoulder.

A man stood at the corner, his dark sunglasses focused on her.

Her knees quivered. They stared at each other, neither moving. This wasn't a normal pedestrian. He was watching her. She forced her legs to move and stumbled up the street, her pace increasing until she was at a sprint.

A male voice shouted "Wait!" behind her, but the word barely penetrated through the fear clouding her mind.

She turned another corner. A small clothing boutique was on her left, and she darted inside. The clerk behind the counter called out a greeting, but Caroline ignored her. She ducked behind a rack of dresses and dug in her purse for her phone.

"Caroline?" Jake's voice was like whiskey over ice, instantly soothing. There was a lot of ambient noise on his end, and he raised his voice. "I was just about to call you. I—"

"Jake." She peered over the clothing rack and out the glass storefront. "Someone's following me."

"What?" His voice went low, deadly. "Where are you?"

She told him her location. "The police just showed me a picture of Brent. They found his body, and now someone's following me and—"

"It's okay," Jake broke in, his voice gentling. "This man following you, is he about six-feet, with sandy-blond hair?"

"What?" She pinched her forehead between her thumb and forefinger. She hadn't thought to get his description. She tried to remember. "Yes? I don't know. Why? What's going on?"

"I'm going to make another call," he said. "Stay on the line."

A minute later he got back to her. "This isn't the way I wanted to tell you, but that man following you is a friend of mine. He's approaching your location now. He's safe."

The man from the street opened the door to the boutique. He raised both his hands in a calming gesture. "Hi, Caroline. My name is Brody. I'm really sorry that I scared you. Jake asked me to keep an eye on you."

She gripped the clothing rack with shaking hands. The adrenaline that had dumped into her system curdled her stomach. "You're having someone follow me?" she hissed at Jake.

"I need to make sure you're safe," he said. "Brody is a member of Delta Squad. I have him and a couple others rotating out, making sure nothing happens to you while you're at work."

Caroline dropped her head to the rack of dresses, fighting against the burn behind her eyes. She didn't know if she was angry or grateful.

Gratitude won out. "So you have a network of guys watching out for me when you can't be there? That's…" The nicest thing anyone had ever done for her. "A relief."

She swallowed. She didn't want it, she'd fought against it, but Jake was the one person who made her feel safe. And that feeling wasn't one she wanted to lose.

Jake bit out a frustrated sigh. "Yes, and unfortunately I'm not going to be there for a little bit."

"What are you talking about?"

Brody fingered a skimpy nightgown arranged on a side table, and she turned away, her stomach sinking.

"My squad got called up," Jake said. "I'm sorry, Caroline, but I'm wheels up in an hour, and I don't know when I'll be back."

Chapter Ten

JAKE DUG HIS KNUCKLES into his thigh, staring at the wall of the C-130 as it flew him and his men over the Atlantic Ocean. He'd never wanted his cell phone so badly. Before he'd left stateside, he'd set up a schedule with their sister squad to watch over Caroline, but his brain kept spinning with worry.

What if Delta got called up, too? It didn't usually happen that the entire special operations team went on missions at the same time, but it wasn't impossible.

What if one of their cars broke down, leaving Caroline unprotected?

What if someone slipped past the night watch and got into her house?

His gut churned. How the fuck did the men with wives or girlfriends handle their relationships and being special forces? He loved his job, but leaving Caroline alone when trouble was at her door? It was killing him.

A rolled-up pair of socks bounced off his face.

Jake glared at Chris, the asshole who'd thrown them. "Want to tell me why you did that?"

"I've been talking to you for a solid two minutes before realizing you weren't even listening." Chris smirked. "Must be thinking about your lady."

Jake scowled. Chris and Ryan were sitting up front with Jake, but he wished they were in the rear catching shut-eye like Tony and Travis. He wanted to be alone with his thoughts.

"Yeah, I'm thinking about her." Jake crossed his arms over his chest. "She has a psychopath on her trail who isn't afraid to put a bullet in someone's head. This op couldn't have come at a worse time."

"We're not wedding planners. We don't get to schedule our work," Chris reminded him.

Jake ground his jaw. He knew that, it had just never been a problem before now.

Ryan leaned forward, resting his forearms on his legs. "If it was Julian Diaz she met, he's dropped off the face of the earth. All of my joyrides into confidential databases are pulling up Jack and shit. He probably went back down to South America to make up with daddy."

"If you were trying to create your own drug empire in the American market, would you turn and flee because one woman saw your face?" Jake scrubbed his hand over his jaw. The expressions on Ryan's and Chris's faces said it all.

Diaz was a threat to Caroline, and Jake wasn't there to protect her.

"You can't do anything about it now," Ryan said. "You need to focus on the job ahead of us. Otherwise you might not get home safe in order to take care of Caroline."

Jake pounded the side of his fist into the wall of the plane, ignoring the sting. "I know, but knowing something and doing it are two very different things."

Chris's face went uncharacteristically serious. "That's what we've been trained to do, man, so suck it up and get your head in the game."

"Which one of you ladies is into sucking head now?" Travis strolled up, stretching his back into an arch. Tony was a step behind.

"Sorry, ladies, we don't have time for fellatio," Tony said. "We need to suit up." He tossed a pack to Jake.

In silence, the men put on their gear, double-checking each other's harnesses. Jake pulled out a map and ran through the plan, and all possible contingencies, for the hundredth time.

For once, Chris was right. He couldn't do anything for Caroline now, but he could do a lot to fuck up his squad if he didn't concentrate. He'd have to trust his fellow Raiders to watch over her.

The aft cargo door grinded open, the inky night sky greeting them with a cold blast of air.

The other squad was just as well trained as his. Jake knew this, just as he knew the other men would risk their lives to protect Caroline. So he had to ignore the queasy feeling in his stomach and press on. Hopefully their part in this shit show they were jumping into would wrap up in under a week. And for that week, his mind and body belonged to his squad.

The men strode to the rear of the plane. "You ready for this?" Ryan asked him, raising his voice to be heard.

Jake held out his hand to give Ryan a fist-bump. "Oorah."

The lights in the plane flashed.

"Hell yeah!" Chris yelled, and with two running steps, leapt headfirst out of the plane.

The other men followed, launching themselves into the open void.

Jake let his training take over, his mind taking on a singular focus as it did at the start of every mission. He packed up his worry for Caroline, stuffed it in a mental box, and left it on the plane as he stepped into darkness.

Chapter Eleven

CAROLINE HEFTED THE BRICK onto her hip and plod-
ded from the corner of her backyard to the low
wall she was building on the other side. She set it
in place then rose, rubbing her back. A boyfriend
would really come in handy on days like this. Someone to help around the house, do the heavy lifting,
give her a nice back massage at the end of the day....

An image of Jake rose in her mind, his handsome
face, his large, rough hands. A boyfriend could also
do other things to her body to help her relax, if he
was good at least.

She had a feeling Jake would be very, very good.

She sighed and went for another brick. *You don't
want to be in a relationship with Jake. He's military.
He'll leave.* She squatted at the edge of the lawn and
placed the brick down, centering it halfway over the
two bricks below. Her stomach twisted in disgust.

Her reasoning was starting to sound thin, even to herself.

But Jake had left. He'd been gone for six days. If she ever needed a reminder why she didn't date military, this was it. She'd only known him a couple of weeks, and her nights were already sleepless with worry for him. Sometime during the second night he'd been gone, her nightmares had transformed from her lost in the middle of the ocean to Jake lost in the desert. Abandoned on a ship. For some reason, her brain had even had him lost in a system of caves. Danger always surrounded him, and there was nothing she could do to stop the inevitable.

She rubbed the back of her neck and stood. Her subconscious really sucked at times. She turned for another brick, then froze.

Jake stood at the corner of her house, looking exhausted and alive and much too sexy for his own good.

Her feet twitched, wanting to run to him, but she forced herself to remain still. "You're back."

He slid his sunglasses to the top of his head. "I'm back. I came straight from base." His gaze drank her in, from her dirty and torn sneakers to the ballcap on her head and everything in between. "No problems while I was away?"

"No problems." Except her heart aching every time she wondered how he was. She strode to the pile next to him and picked up another brick. "In fact, it's been so quiet I decided to get onto a project I'd been dragging my feet on."

Jake wrapped his arm around her waist and tugged her close. He held her loosely, seemingly content to just hold her, and dropped his temple to her head.

She wanted to lean into him, wrap him up tight, but she couldn't let herself cling. His disappearing act the last few days had shown her that. Not that he hadn't left for a good reason or that he'd had a choice. But still. She couldn't rely on him.

With one last squeeze, Jake pressed a kiss to the top of her head then took the brick from her hand and picked up two more. "A retaining wall?"

She grabbed another brick and followed after him, placing her block in its row on the wall. "Yep, although it's only decorative. It's not retaining anything." While her mom had been sick, the yard had gone to hell. Slowly, she'd been trying to beautify her spaces again.

She turned, her breath catching as Jake sank down and added his bricks to her wall. Nothing she had done had improved her backyard's appearance as much as having Jake in it. Stubble dusted his jaw, making him look even more deadly, and the polo shirt he wore only emphasized his hard body.

Her belly fluttered. It almost hurt to look at him, he was that handsome. He was like the sun, something dangerous to stare at directly.

A sun she wanted to lick.

He glanced around. "Where's your adhesive?"

"I'm not using one." She gave her head a tiny shake and refocused on her project. Unlike looking at Jake, the brick wall didn't give her tingles in places that had absolutely no right to tingle. Her wall was at three bricks high, and she thought she'd only go up one more row. The curving wall around her lawn gave her yard a bit more elegance, but was still low enough for her to step over to tend to the trees behind.

"And you didn't dig a trench for the bottom row." Jake stood. "This looks great, but it's unstable. If a kid comes along and walks on it, it will fall over."

"I don't have kids."

"Not yet." He gave her a look. She couldn't quite identify it, but it had her belly doing a slow backflip. "Things change," he said. "I'll get some silicone and stabilize it."

Caroline pressed her palms against her thighs. Everything about Jake Skinner was designed to provoke. She was used to being even-keeled. Self-possessed. Zen-like even. But Jake knew how to push all her buttons. The ones that lit up her body, thawed her heart... and sparked her temper.

"I don't have children now, so the wall is fine." But she would have to remember not to sit on the wall herself. If she took a spill, she'd never be able to look him in the eye again.

Jake covered a yawn. "It will save you time in the future if you do it right now. And we don't want a kid to get hurt."

"You're worried about a hypothetical child?" A pulse started to beat behind her temple.

"A future likelihood." He pulled out his phone and started searching. "There's a hardware store not far from here. I'll—"

She plucked his phone from his hand. "You're not gluing my wall together." Had it just been minutes ago she'd wanted a boyfriend to help her with housework? Her mouth went dry. And why was he talking about kids? They'd just flippin' met. Her heart beat erratically. She would not freak about this. She. Would. Not.

He took his phone back and slid it in his back pocket. "It won't take but a minute."

"I'm not objecting because of the time involved." She stomped to the sliding glass door that led to her kitchen.

"Then what is your objection?" Jake followed behind her, sounding much too reasonable and unperturbed for her liking.

"That... because..." She threw up her hands. "I don't have kids, there aren't any hints of them on the horizon, and I'm not going to childproof my home on the off-chance one might appear in the future!"

He reached around her and slid open the door. "One thing I've learned in special forces is that a hypothetical can become reality right quick." He arched an eyebrow as she glared at him.

She brushed past him and went to the sink to wash her hands. She could see it. Them living together, a little boy with Jake's intense eyes and her light hair.

She could see it, and it scared the bejeezus out of her.

She snatched a towel from the handle of her fridge and dried her hands vigorously enough to remove skin. "I'm not having kids with you, Jake."

"Not if you don't want them." He leaned against the counter and crossed one ankle over the other.

"I'm not getting into a relationship with you either. I've told you that."

He hooked a finger in the waistband of her shorts as she tried to pass by. He reeled her close. "I'd never do anything to make you uncomfortable, but there's something here. Something good. And I'm not going to let your fear keep us apart."

"That isn't really something you have control over." She bit her lip. She didn't want to live in fear. How many good things in life had she let pass her by because she was too scared to take a chance? Was Jake worth taking a chance on?

"You might be surprised at what I can control." He lowered his head, his breath dancing over her skin.

He brushed his lips over the shell of her ear. "And at how much you might like it."

A shiver started at the base of her spine and rolled out through her body. She inhaled deeply, enveloped in his masculine scent. He smelled of soap and spice and everything she'd ever wanted. His heat, his touch, everything about Jake swamped her senses.

Her muscles sagged, and she pressed her head into his shoulder. She was tired. Of fighting this, fighting him. Of running scared. She'd sworn she'd never date someone in the military, and now this Marine was the only man she wanted. Her mom would have split her sides laughing at this twist of fate.

She wrapped her arms around his waist and pressed the side of her head to his chest. His heart beat a steady thump, his warmth soaking into her bones. "I'm glad you're safe," she whispered.

"Ditto."

She sucked in a deep breath, gathering her courage. She could do this. She could take a chance. Rolling onto her toes, Caroline brought her face within inches of Jake's. She cupped his jaw, rubbing her palm against the soft bristle of his scruff. "Jake, will you—"

He didn't wait until she finished the question. He closed the distance and covered her mouth with his own.

Caroline sighed at the rightness of it. Jake held her like he was never letting her go, and any lingering fears that he would abandon her withered and died.

He nibbled at her bottom lip and slid his hand up the back of her tank top.

Her skin flushed beneath his touch. She teased his mouth open, then deepened the kiss. It went from sweet to scorching in one second flat.

Jake lifted her to sit on the counter, wedging his hips between her thighs as his tongue sparred with hers.

She reached for the hem of his polo, tugged at the fabric when it stuck at his arms. "Up," she demanded.

Jake groaned, and pressed his forehead to hers. "Sweetheart, you know how badly I want you."

Caroline wriggled her hips, feeling his hard length pressed against her groin. "Yes, I can tell." She nipped at his jaw.

Jake leaned back, putting altogether too much space between them. "I want to do this right. I don't want to screw you on the kitchen counter, at least not for our first time. You deserve dinner, some romance."

She yanked on his shirt, but he didn't budge. "I'm not hungry, and if I want romance I'll rewatch a Nora Ephron movie."

He took her hand from his polo and kissed her palm. "You deserve more. I don't want to mess this up. I can't." The expression in his eyes slayed her. It was a look of pure devotion. Her heart stuttered. In that moment, she'd do anything for this man. Even indulge his silly notions about doing things right.

She blew out a breath and slid off the counter. "Fine. Dinner first. But you're not going to talk me out of dessert." She ran her finger down his chest, so he knew just what it was she wanted on the menu.

Jake chuckled. "Go take a shower or get changed or whatever it is you need to get ready. I'll be waiting for you."

Caroline hurried into her room and set the world's record for fastest shower by a woman. She discarded a pair of tight jeans and a skirt before settling on a cute and flirty dress. She pulled her hair into a ponytail, too eager to style it properly, slapped on some makeup and was out her bedroom door in fifteen minutes flat.

She hurried to the living room, only to find Jake sacked out on her sofa, his head lolling on the backrest, one leg kicked up onto her coffee table. He breathed, slow and steady, sleeping so soundly Caroline didn't even have the heart to rouse him to move to a more comfortable location.

She stood and watched him for an embarrassingly long time. This man was going to change her life. She felt it in her soul. She just didn't know if she'd come out of the transformation a broken woman, or the happiest one alive.

Kicking out of her heels, she went to find a blanket and carefully draped it over him. The poor man was exhausted. She ran her fingers through his hair. And the first thing he'd done when he'd got back was to come see her.

She swallowed. He was going to ruin her for all other men.

Sighing, she pushed off the arm of the sofa and padded to the kitchen. If they weren't going out to dinner, the least she could do was have something hot waiting for Jake when he woke up.

Chapter Twelve

JAKE'S BODY TENSED AS he blinked awake. Without moving, he assessed his situation. On a couch, not his own, in a darkened room.

Caroline's house.

But what had woken him?

He was easing out from under a soft, microfiber blanket when he heard the sound again.

A feminine whimper sounded down the hall.

Jake rolled to his feet and made it to Caroline's room in under two seconds. The door was cracked, and he pushed it wider. A shaft of moonlight angled through the cracked blinds, revealing a single lump in the middle of the bed.

The lump shifted, accompanied by another sign of distress.

"Caroline," Jake said in a low voice. He sat on the edge of her mattress and rubbed her shoulder. "Sweetheart, you're having a bad dream."

Her arm flailed out.

He caught it before it clipped his jaw and shook her a little harder. "Caroline, wake up."

Her body went stiff, then relaxed into his hands. "Jake?"

He helped her sit. "I'm here. You were having a bad dream."

She settled against his chest as though it was the most natural thing in the world, her body relaxing against his.

His lungs expanded. When he held Caroline, he felt content like he never had before. It felt right. He wanted to be the man to comfort her in the middle of the night, although he hated that she had nightmares and probably would for years to come.

"Do you want to talk about your dream?" he asked.

She shook her head, her hair scraping against his shirt.

He brushed it back away from her face. "Are you sure? Sometimes talking about it takes the sting out of the fear."

She wrapped her arms around his waist and squeezed him tight. "It doesn't matter. You're here now. Safe."

He tilted his head. "Was your nightmare about me?"

"Does it matter?" She sighed. "It wasn't real. Besides, I'm getting used to them. Except for the couple of days you spent at my house before you left, I've had nightmares every night. I think my body knows I'm safe when you're around, but that's why tonight my subconscious decided to put you in danger."

He cupped the back of her head. "You know I can take care of myself. And the men on the squad, we all take care of each other. You don't have to worry about me."

"I know," she said, but it didn't sound like she believed it.

He rubbed the small of her back. Her thin tank top was no barrier for the heat of her skin. "Have you thought more about talking to someone?" He swallowed, a bitter taste in the back of his throat. "You went through something no woman should ever have to."

Caroline turned and rolled to her knees. She placed a finger over his lips. "Like I said, when you're here with me, I'm not scared for myself." She traced his mouth with the pad of her index finger. "And as for being scared for you when you leave on a mission, well, that's just something I'm going to have to come to terms with, isn't it?"

He stilled, barely breathing. "Does that mean you've given up on your no-military-men nonsense?"

Her smile was barely visible in the dim light. "I wouldn't call it nonsense. I had very good reasons for it. But yes, I'm giving up on it. I don't want to miss out on you, Jake. I don't want to miss out on what this might be."

Elation burbled in his chest. With a rough shout of victory, he tumbled them both onto the bed, rolling until she was on top of him. He kissed her chin. Her throat. "I have tomorrow off. We'll go for a big breakfast, or brunch, whatever you want. We'll spend the whole day together, like a real date."

She shifted, settling her thighs around his hips. Her plush breasts pressed against his chest. "Can we pretend we had our date last night?" She rolled her hips, her heat teasing his cock.

He groaned. "You know I want to do things right, even if that means taking it slow."

She rolled those damn hips again, this time in a tantalizing circle. "Oh, we can take it very, *very* slow." She sucked his earlobe into her mouth, sending sparks of desire straight to his groin. "This feels right," she whispered. "Please, don't make me wait. I want you now."

Jake ground his teeth. How was he expected to do the right thing when Caroline was temptation personified? He flipped their positions, pinning her to the mattress. But then, as she said, this did feel right. And he'd been trained to recognize the perfect moment to strike.

He took her mouth, their tongues tangling. Between her eager hands and his, their clothes didn't stand a chance. In moments, he had her body bare beneath his, ripe for the plucking.

He skimmed his lips down her throat and into the valley between her breasts. She shuddered as he licked each curve. Her scent, her taste exploded across his senses. He inched lower, his fingertips grazing over her hip and thigh to pull her leg wide.

Caroline gripped his hair, her fingers digging into his scalp at the first swipe of his tongue across her slit.

"So wet," he murmured. He opened her to his gaze and took another taste. "So good."

Her hips rocked into his face as he took his fill. She moaned, her breath shuddering, as he took her higher. "Jake... Oh, God..."

Easing a finger into her channel, he sucked her clit between his lips, drawing hard.

Her back arched as she came. Her cries filled the room, swelling Jake with a primal surge of satisfaction. He'd done that to her. He'd satisfied his woman. And he wanted to do it every damn night of his life. He couldn't imagine anywhere better than being between Caroline's thighs.

He pumped his fingers in and out of her, easing her down from her climax before building her right back up. His cock ached as it rubbed against the bedsheets. He gave her nub one last kiss before crawling up her body.

Caroline wrapped her arms around his back, spreading her legs wider in invitation.

It was one he couldn't refuse. With a groan, he notched the head of his cock at her entrance and pushed his way into heaven.

The last clinging tendrils of her nightmare disappeared. There was no room for fear or worry, not when she was filled with Jake.

He stilled deep inside of her and brushed a lock of hair off her forehead. His eyes were dark in the moonlight, but his gaze was as intense as ever.

"You okay?" he asked.

She was so okay it scared her. A person wasn't supposed to fall this hard, this fast. In answer, she lifted her head and brushed her lips over his.

Jake rested on his forearms, framing her face with his large hands. He sucked her bottom lip into his mouth as he started to move.

Jake's love-making was as single-minded as everything else about him. His thrusts were long and even. He slowly built her body up until she was scraping her nails down his back in frustration.

She wrapped her legs around his thighs, trying to increase the pace.

Jake merely chuckled and nuzzled her throat.

"Faster," she said, breathless.

"Not yet." He cut off her protest with another slow, drugging kiss. When they broke apart, she was light-headed.

"Jake." She arched her back, trying to get impossibly closer. He felt like a part of her, one she hadn't even known she'd been missing. Sweat dampened his chest, and she licked a bead from his skin. "Please."

He muttered a curse. Rising higher on his knees, Jake drove into her. His cock stretched her core, and there was a delicious pinch each time he bottomed out. She'd never had sex like this before, not with a man who seemed to know just what her body craved.

His pants mingled with her whimpers. Her bed frame slapped against the wall. Tingles started at the base of her spine and spread through her body, puckering her nipples and making her sheath grip at his length.

"That's it, sweetheart." He took the back of her knee and opened her farther. His next stroke had her mewling. "Come for me."

He hammered into her, faster, harder, until her vision blurred and her mind went white with pleasure. She cried out as wave after wave of ecstasy cascaded through her body.

Jake's pace never faltered. He surged past her grasping muscles, extending her pleasure as he chased his own release. With a husky growl, he planted himself deep inside and rolled his hips as he came.

Spurts of liquid heat filled her, and she pulled him close, sighing with contentment. That was something else they'd done out of order, having sex first then telling him she was on birth control later, but she couldn't regret their impulsiveness. She loved feeling him skin to skin, and she trusted him implicitly to keep her safe.

Jake rolled to his side, pulling her with him so they were chest to chest. His heavy breathing gusted across her cheek as their bodies cooled.

This was the part where she should start freaking out. She'd thrown all her rules out and given herself, heart and soul, to a man who could disappear on a moment's notice.

She trailed her fingers through the springy curls on his chest. The panic never came. Being with Jake didn't just feel right in the heat of lust, it felt right all the time.

"You'll stay?" she asked.

He huffed and pulled her tight. "Of course."

Snuggling into him, she closed her eyes. Sleep pulled at her, and she let herself fall under its spell. The last thing she heard was Jake whispering, "Sweet dreams."

Chapter Thirteen

CAROLINE'S FINGERS WERE TANGLED tightly within his as they strolled down the sidewalk. She'd wanted to spend the day in the nearby tourist town of Swansboro, and Jake was more than happy to oblige. She'd dragged him into every cutesy antique store and boutique they'd passed, an activity he knew his guys would rib him about.

Jake couldn't care less. He looked down at Caroline. Her light blonde hair skimmed her bare shoulders, swinging with every step. She wore a snug tank top over a brightly-colored flowing skirt. She looked good enough to eat.

She could have asked him to take her to a knitting class, and he would have bought his own set of needles. Caroline had him wrapped around her little finger and she didn't even know it.

She paused in front of a large glass window that had flowers and leaves painted around its edges.

"That pot belly stove would look great in my garden as a planter." She pointed at the cast iron stove that had been painted a rustic turquoise.

"Not quite its intended function." Jake shrugged. "But high points for creativity."

She nudged him with her shoulder. "I think the fact that the base has rusted out prevents it from being used as an oven." She bent down and squinted at the tag attached to the item. "Well, creative or not, it's not in my budget." She chewed on her lower lip. "I do have to buy new tires soon. Instead of paying the recycling fee on the old ones, I'll do something with those in the garden instead."

Jake straightened. "Your tires are worn?" He shook his head. "You shouldn't be driving around on those. When we get back, I'll—"

"They're fine." She took his hand and tugged him down the sidewalk. "They just have a bit of miles on them. I have been taking care of things like new tires all by myself for a while now, you know."

He rubbed his knuckle against his breastbone. He knew. And he appreciated how independent and competent Caroline was. As someone who could be away from home weeks at a time, he would need a self-sufficient woman. Didn't mean he wasn't going to worry or that he didn't want to help her take care of those little things.

He slung his arm over her shoulders. Her skin was warm from the sun, and she notched perfectly into his side. He kissed the top of her head. "I know you can handle things yourself, but that doesn't mean you can't lean on me some. Lighten your load." And no matter what she said, he would definitely check out those tires when they got back to her place.

"Hey, I let you pay for lunch." She licked her bottom lip, as if remembering the taste of the spicy arrabiata penne dish they'd eaten. "That's leaning."

"It's a good first step," he agreed.

They turned down the street where he'd parked and passed in front of the public library. A bulletin board sat below the American flag, and Caroline headed for it. "I love this library. They've had some great author signings here before, but I'm not seeing anything coming up." She bit her lip, tracing her fingers over a flyer.

"They're hiring," Jake said, reading the notice. A black Escalade turned the corner and came toward them at a Sunday-afternoon pace. The hairs on the back of his neck rose as he tried to peer through the tinted windows to the occupants inside but could see nothing. Subtly, he shifted his body in front of Caroline's, not relaxing until the vehicle drove past.

"Assistant librarian," Caroline said lightly. "It must be nice to work with books instead of numbers."

The Escalade turned down the next street, and he refocused on Caroline. Until Diaz was eliminated, Jake would probably be seeing threats to Caroline everywhere. "Why don't you apply?" he asked.

She rolled her eyes. "I'm sure they're looking for someone with no experience in the field who never finished her English degree."

"That's why you'd be an assistant," he pointed out. "To get experience from the head librarian." He knew Caroline wasn't thrilled with her current job. She'd been forced to take it when her mom was sick. He couldn't imagine going into a nine-to-five job every day that he didn't like.

Scratch that. He couldn't imagine having a nine-to-five-job period. But it was the reality for most people, and Caroline shouldn't be wasting forty hours of her week doing something she didn't love.

"Go on." He unpinned the flyer and handed it to her. "It doesn't hurt to apply."

She pressed her lips together and pinned the paper back on the board. "It also pays less than what I'm currently making. I can't afford it, no matter how great it sounds."

"You could afford it if we moved in together." Jake blinked. He hadn't thought about those words before he'd said them.

He rolled them around in his brain.

Living with Caroline.

Seeing her face every morning. Holding her tight each night. Laughing with her at the dinner table.

Everything inside of him settled. It sounded...good.

Her mouth dropped open. "Move in together? We just had sex—" She broke off as two older women toddled past, books clutched in their hands. Caroline blushed. "We just slept together for the first time last night," she hissed at him. "Don't you think you're moving a little fast?"

"I like fast." He placed his hands on her hips and tugged her close. "I've never felt this way about anyone before. I don't want to waste time."

"But...." She shook her head. "I have my house, my mom's house. I don't know if I'm ready to—"

He bent and placed a kiss on her lips. "I can move in with you, if you want to stay there. Take on some of the bills, help you build that retaining wall so it doesn't fall over at the first breeze."

She slapped his chest, giving him a look he was coming to adore. Like he was impossible and wonderful all wrapped into one.

And she hadn't said no.

"Can I think about it?" she asked.

"Of course. Take all the time you need." His chest filled. He was going to be living with Caroline soon. He saw the outcome as clearly as he saw her standing before him. "Just know that whatever your decision, I'm not going anywhere."

She beamed at him, her smile so beautiful it made something inside of him ache.

"I can't believe I had a rule against military men." She pulled out of his arms and dug in her purse for her phone. She snapped a picture of the flyer with the assistant librarian information. "I could have had some sweetie being this nice to me for years."

Jake growled. "Other military men are all dogs. They weren't right for you." He wrapped his arms around her again. He couldn't imagine how he would have felt if she'd been with someone else when he'd first met her. He swallowed. If she'd been married.

Were there men out there who found the loves of their lives, only to learn that they weren't available? His gut churned at the thought.

Well, there'd be no slacking on his part. If he wanted to keep Caroline, and he did, he just had to make sure that she was the happiest, most satisfied woman alive. That was his new mission. And he never failed.

He turned them back down the sidewalk the way they'd come. "Now, how about we go back to that ice cream shop you were eyeballing. There's a waffle cone with your name on it."

Chapter Fourteen

CAROLINE RAN HER GAZE down the computer screen, double- and triple-checking her resume one last time. She'd been... *creatively* plumping up her skill set for the past hour. It looked good. Well, as good as it was going to get anyways.

But was it good enough? Chewing on her bottom lip, she pulled up the library's website. She couldn't imagine working somewhere surrounded by books instead of actuarial charts. She had no qualifications for that job beyond two years of an unfinished English degree and a semester working in her college's library reshelving books part-time.

Janice, her coworker in the adjoining cubicle, dropped her face in her hands and cursed. "I hate this program."

Caroline rolled her chair over. She pressed three keys to unlock the screen. "It's sensitive. You just have to know how to talk to it."

Janice blew out a breath. "I never thought I'd be talking to computers all day. When will they start talking back? It will make my life a lot easier."

Caroline flattened her voice into her best Hal impersonation from *2001: A Space Odyssey*. "I'm sorry, Janice. I'm afraid I can't do that. Yet." Laughing, she rolled back to her desk as Janice threw a paper clip at her.

Caroline had never thought she'd be calculating death rates and spending all day looking at a screen, either. But that was life. She tapped her fingers on her desk and glanced at her resume again. But maybe she could make her life a little better. She addressed an email to the hiring manager of the library, attached her resume and cover sheet, and hit send before she could overthink it.

As Jake said, it couldn't hurt to throw her hat in the ring. Even if she got the job, that didn't mean she had to accept the position. It paid less than what she was currently making. If she did take it, she would have to get a roommate.

A slow tingle started at the base. of her neck and danced down her spine. Moving in with Jake would be crazy. They'd only known each other for a couple of weeks. People didn't just move in with guys they'd just met. Yet....

Even though the idea was crazy, it didn't *feel* crazy to her.

An email pinged in her inbox, and Caroline forced her mind back to business. She spent the rest of the afternoon responding to questions and cleaning up reports. The office slowly emptied out, but Caroline kept working. She had to make up for the time she'd spent on her personal business.

Her desk phone rang. She jerked, startled. The sound was loud in the silence. Blinking, she tried to refocus her bleary eyes. "Hello?" she asked absently into the receiver. She squinted at the number at the bottom of her column. That couldn't be right.

"Hello?" she repeated. There was no answer but quiet breathing. Caroline straightened in her chair, her shoulders slowly going back. Someone was on the line. He hadn't hung up. If the last couple weeks of her life hadn't happened, she would have thought it was just some kid having fun.

But the last couple weeks of her life had happened, and now she saw danger everywhere. She gently lowered the receiver and hung up the phone as if it was a bomb that had to be treated delicately. She took three even breaths, trying to get her heart rate to even out.

People got crank calls all the time. Hell, it could have been a salesman. Sometimes, they called the next person on their list while still talking to their current mark. It didn't have to mean anything. Still, she'd tell Jake about it when he picked her up.

She stood and looked around her office. Only two other people remained in the large, open space. Caroline didn't want to be the last person left in the building. She grabbed her cell phone and texted Jake that she was ready. She hadn't liked the idea when he'd said he'd take her to work and pick her up today, but she was happy to be avoiding the dark parking garage now.

She gathered her things, said goodbye to the remaining stragglers, and went down to wait in the lobby. The building housed the offices of several companies. A security guard manned a front desk, but his main duty was to direct visitors to the right office. He wasn't armed, but Caroline gratefully went to chat with him while she waited.

They were discussing the disappointing season the Panthers had when Jake's SUV rolled to a stop in front of the glass doors. "Have a good night," Caroline said to the guard before hurrying outside.

She smiled when Jake got out of the vehicle and opened the passenger door for her. There was a light drizzle, and the ends of Jake's hair curled in the damp. She rolled onto her toes and kissed him. "You shouldn't get out of the car when it's raining, silly."

"You call this rain?" He smiled, but it didn't reach his eyes. He helped her inside and circled back to the driver's seat. "How was your day?" he asked, pulling into traffic.

"Fine."

"Your car is back at your house, with new tires," he said.

"Thanks. I appreciate you taking it in for me." She turned in her seat to examine him. Jake's shoulders weren't as upright as normal, and he looked bone-tired. "What's wrong?"

He pulled up to a red light and gripped the back of his neck. "There was a terrorist attack on a base in Kenya today. Eight men died."

"Oh, Jake." Caroline rested her hand above his knee and squeezed. "Were they Marines?"

"Six of them." The light turned green, and he drove forward. "The other two were Army."

The back of her throat burned. "Does this mean you're going to be leaving?"

He glanced at her, his lips lifting in a small smile. "Probably not, but I know every man wants to go hunt down the assholes."

She nodded. The small kernel of dread she seemed to carry in her stomach ever since she'd fallen for Jake bloomed. She was dating a man with a dangerous job. He wanted to put himself in danger if it would help his fellow servicemen. It was one of the reasons she loved him. It was a huge part of who Jake was.

It scared the hell out of her.

She hated the risks he took. She didn't know if she'd ever sleep peacefully again if she stayed with this man.

"Are you tired?" he asked.

She dragged her mind from her dark thoughts. "Not really. Why?"

"When something like this happens, the squad and I like to meet and have a drink in the fallen servicemen's honor. Would you mind if we went to *The Limber Ginger*?"

"Of course not." She rubbed his leg. How many times had his friends gathered together to raise a drink to a fellow Marine? If something happened to Jake and his men when they were on a secret mission, would they receive the same honor? Would anyone ever know what happened to them? Would she?

Her cell phone beeped. Caroline dug it out of her purse. It reminded her of her strange phone calls, but now wasn't the right time to tell Jake about them. "It's Sam. She wants to know what I'm doing tonight," she told Jake as she read the text. "Do you mind if I tell her where we're going?"

"Not at all. Your friends are always welcome with me and my men."

The rest of the drive to the bar was made in silence, and their solemn moods were mirrored by the atmosphere in the bar. It seemed as though everyone knew of the incident, and *The Limber Ginger* was quieter than Caroline had ever seen it.

Jake nodded to Kieran who was planted behind the bar. The owner reached out a meaty hand and shook Jake's. "I'm sorry for your compatriots," he said. "Everything's half off for servicemen tonight."

"Thanks." Jake jerked his chin at a large round table near the center of the bar. "And thanks for that, too. It's appreciated."

Caroline frowned, looking at the table. It was empty except for eight full mugs of beer.

Kieran ran his fingers through his beard. "The least I could do."

A waitress came up with an order, and with a nod to Jake and Caroline, Kieran grabbed a glass and turned for the tap.

Jake clasped her hand and led her to a table in the corner where his squad sat. He pulled out a chair for her then sat down by her side.

Caroline pointed at the large round table. "What's that about?"

"Tradition." Ryan grabbed two beers from the center of their table and pushed them in front of Jake and Caroline.

Caroline wrapped her hands around the cold glass. "Oh." Eight glasses for the eight fallen. The backs of her eyes burned, and she blinked away the tears. Sometimes life just sucked. "Did you guys know them?"

"Viper did." Travis picked a French fry from his plate then tossed it back down. No hint of his trademark humor lit his face.

Tony nodded. "Lance Corporal McGinnis. We were in basic together."

"Oh," Caroline said. The rest of the men just stared into their beers. She couldn't think of one thing to say to help them. Instead, she scooted her chair closer to Jake and rested her head on his shoulder.

"Jeez, who died in here?" Sam strode up, shrugging out of her jacket. She grabbed an empty chair and pulled it up next to Caroline's, wedging herself between her and Ryan. "I've been in churches more rocking than this place tonight."

Chris narrowed his blue eyes. "Congratulations, you read the room correctly. Too bad you had to ruin your observation by opening your mouth. How about a little tact next time?"

Sam's jaw dropped. "Excuse me? Who the hell are you to talk to me that way?" She glanced around the table. "In fact, just who are you?"

Caroline placed a hand on her friend's arm. "Sam, this is Chris Gunn, the last member of Jake's squad. You didn't get to meet him before."

Sam glared at the man in question. "Not a great loss."

Chris's eyes flared. "This is Caroline's friend, Sam?" He ran a hand through his black hair and huffed. "Your description of her was way off, brother," he said to Travis.

Jake raised his hand. "Ease up, Chris, she doesn't know. And Sam, you'll have to excuse all of us tonight. We had some bad news."

Caroline leaned over and told Sam what had happened. Her friend's eyes went damp when she looked at the beer mugs at the next table, but when they landed back on Chris, they were still spitting flames.

Sam had many wonderful traits, but being quick to forgive wasn't one of them.

Travis waved down a waitress. "How about something to eat and drink?" he asked Sam, smiling. "We might not be the most fun tonight, but we can still treat you right. Not all of us have lost our manners."

Chris glared at him. The edges of Travis's lips twitched, but he otherwise ignored his friend.

They broke into separate conversations. Sam told Travis stories from her lifeguard days in high school. Tony chatted with Chris and Ryan about memories from boot camp. Caroline just sat quietly with Jake, resting her head on his shoulder, tucking her hand snug between his arm and ribs.

He was still with her. Jake was still alive, and warm, and wonderful. The saying that life is short was so trite, yet so true. Even if Jake never faced another battle in his life, he would still grow old and die. Just like she would. So much of her life had dealt with sickness and death. She was tired of it. She wanted to live.

She ran her hand over Jake's T-shirt and rested it over his heart. It thumped softly against her palm. "Whenever you're ready, take me home, Jake."

He gazed down at her, his eyes soft. "Need something, sweetheart?"

She cupped his cheek. "Right now, all I need is you."

Chapter Fifteen

JAKE GRIPPED THE BACK of Caroline's head, drawing out the kiss.

"I'm going to be late," she murmured.

He sucked on her lower lip, not really caring at the moment that he was running behind, too. Being with Caroline was like having a fire kindled inside of him. He wanted her all the time. The memories of the night before lingered.

Caroline sighed, and, regretfully, Jake pulled back. Pedestrians strode past his SUV, cups of coffee in their hands and aggravated expressions on their faces. Jake could relate. He'd already been out for his morning PT with his men and then back for breakfast with Caroline, but he had more on his schedule for the day. And making out like a teenager in the front seat wasn't on his to-do list. Sadly.

"Text me when you want to get picked up."

She nodded and flipped the visor down in front of her, reapplying her lipstick. "It should be a little earlier today. If you can't get me, I'm sure Sam can."

"I'll be here," he said. They hadn't talked anymore about moving in together, and he wanted to impress upon her that she could count on him for anything.

She reached for the door handle then paused. Eyes locked, they leaned toward each other.

With a groan, Jake turned his head and kissed her cheek. If they locked lips again, she was never getting to work. "Have a good day," he said.

Nodding, she hopped out of the car and into her office building.

Jake watched her say hello to the guard behind the front desk before putting his SUV in gear. He rolled a foot forward then stomped on the brake. "Damn." He threw the gear into park and grabbed Caroline's cell phone from the cupholder. He got out of the vehicle and trotted after her.

She was pushing the call button for the elevator when he hit the lobby.

"Caroline," he called, striding toward her. "You forgot...."

A shadow peeled from the wall, creeping down the hallway next to the elevator. The figure reached into its jacket pocket. Metal flashed.

Time slowed. Stretched.

Caroline turned, her movements appearing lethargic. Every strand of her hair came into focus as it swung out about her face. Her lips stretched into a smile when she saw him.

Jake's ears buzzed. The chime from the elevator arriving sounded dim, muffled, as though he heard it through a pool of water. His feet started flying before he even fully realized the threat.

Caroline's eyes widened a moment before his body crashed into hers. He took her down in a tumble of arms and legs as a shot rang out. He rolled her body toward the elevator's open doors and shoved her inside the cab.

Screams rang out in the lobby. The figure turned and ran.

"Jake!" Caroline clung to him.

He pressed her back to the side of the elevator, out of the line of sight. And fire. "Get between floors one and two then hit the emergency stop." He jumped to his feet. "Wait for me. Don't open the doors 'til you hear my voice."

He waited for her nod before turning and racing after the assailant. A woman in a business suit was just clambering to her feet fifteen feet to his right on the sidewalk. He sidestepped around her. A car door slammed. Tires screeched.

Jake caught a glimpse of a man's profile in the passenger seat. He pounded after the car, darting into the street and weaving his way around the slow morning traffic. The car, a dark blue Acura, slowed at the corner to make a right turn.

Jake put on a burst of speed. He grabbed the passenger side door and yanked it open. Hanging onto the roof and door, he lifted his feet and let the momentum of the car carry him forward. His shoes scrambled to find purchase on the bottom frame.

The shooter snarled up at him, elbowing him in the gut.

Jake punched his face. His knuckles burned, but he hit him again, the crack of bone on bone the most satisfying sound he'd heard in a long time.

The shooter raised his pistol, and Jake grabbed the man's wrist, knocking it against the dashboard.

Cursing in Spanish, the driver reached for his own piece. He pointed the muzzle at Jake's head.

Jake gripped the collar of the guy in the passenger seat and fell backwards, trying to bring the asshole out with him. His shoulder twisted, straining to stay in its socket. The man's shirt jerked out of Jake's hand, and he tumbled to the pavement. He rolled, but the impact still jolted through him.

He pushed to his feet, chest heaving. The shooter was hanging halfway out the car door, the seatbelt strap the only thing keeping him from eating asphalt. He pulled himself upright and slammed the door closed as the car sped away.

A horn blared behind Jake, tires squealing.

Jake jumped backwards, landing on a parked car. He pounded the hood. "Damn it." Pulling out his phone, he dialed 9-1-1, keeping it brief. Then he called Ryan.

"I need a license plate ID'd. Now."

Ryan didn't even ask why. He took the numbers and letters and started typing, the frenzied clicking of his keyboard loud across the line. "You do know eventually we might get in trouble for hacking into government databases," he said casually.

"It won't be today." Jake pressed his hand to his sore ribs and hurried back down the sidewalk towards Caroline's building. "What kind of asshole puts on his seatbelt after trying to kill a person?" he muttered.

"Uh, is this a rhetorical question?"

Jake scowled but didn't bother answering his friend. He'd pulled the same maneuver on a perp in Mogadishu, but that douche bag had at least had the decency to come out of the car with Jake when he'd pulled him. An assassin following the seatbelt law was new, and frankly, annoying.

"Got it," Ryan said as Jake pushed through the glass doors. The lobby was deserted except for the security guard huddled behind the front desk speaking into his walkie.

Jake nodded at him as he hurried to the elevator. "Name?" he said into his phone.

"Mr. Pagani. He's a 77-year-old retiree from a dry cleaning business and lives in Raleigh."

"Damn it." Jake stared at the elevator doors. Of course, the car or the plates were stolen. He really hadn't expected anything less, but still, the dead-end stung. "Find any video footage you can on the street that Caroline's office building is on and the street the next block up. The shooter turned right on it." He gave Ryan a description of the car and the men and prayed a random ATM camera had caught something.

Ryan blew out a breath. "I'm good with computers, but I'm not a professional hacker. This might take a while."

"Understood."

"Is Caroline all right?"

The lights above the elevator flickered between 1 and 2. Every possible scenario ran through Jake's head. What if Caroline hadn't left her phone in his vehicle, or he hadn't seen it until too late? What if he'd been one second slower in taking her to the ground?

What if he'd had to watch as her life slipped out of her?

Jake cleared his throat. "She's fine." His toe nudged a bit of metal and plastic. Bending, he swiped up Caroline's cellphone and looked at the elevator again. "Get back to me when you have something," he said and hung up.

"Any way to recall this elevator?" he asked the security guard.

The kid shrugged. "Not any way that I know. If there's a problem, I call the elevator company."

"Perfect," Jake muttered. Caroline didn't have her phone, and without it, there was no way for him to call her to tell her to release the emergency hold.

He blew out a breath, his heartbeat finally starting to slow.

Diaz had tried to kill Caroline. Again. Her being in danger was no longer a hypothetical.

Rage swirled in Jake's gut. If this asshole thought he could hurt his woman and get away with it, he had a harsh lesson coming his way. As of now, Caroline was going into hard protection. He didn't care if she didn't like it; Diaz wouldn't get another shot.

He slid her phone into his pocket then dug his fingertips into the crack of the elevator doors. Slowly, he wedged them open wide enough so he could call up. "Caroline," he shouted. "It's Jake. Bring the elevator back down, sweetheart."

Chapter Sixteen

CAROLINE BLINKED AT THE afternoon sun. She'd thought it would be dark. It felt like they had been in the police station all day.

Jake pulled her into his side. His gaze cut across the parking lot, assessing. He nodded, then led her down the front steps of the station and to his SUV. He opened the door for her, guided her inside, and snapped her seatbelt into place.

Caroline stared at her hands, her mind numb. The silence felt heavy, awkward, when Jake slipped behind the wheel. Silence between them had never been awkward.

"You'd think it would get easier the second time someone shot at you," she said lightly.

Jake shot her a dark look.

Okay, so she wasn't a comedian, but she should at least get points for trying.

He gripped the steering wheel. "Why didn't you tell me you were getting hang up phone calls?"

She sagged back in her seat. "I was going to last night. But your fellow servicemen had died, and we were honoring them at the bar, and it seemed like the wrong time. And then," she said, raising her hand palm up, "I forgot."

A muscle in his jaw ticked. "Don't forget something like that again."

Caroline turned and looked out the window as he started the car. It wasn't as though she'd meant to be reckless. This situation was hardly her fault. She rubbed her breastbone. But she'd seen the tension in his face, the fear and the relief when the elevator doors had opened and he'd pulled her into his arms.

She shouldn't have forgotten to tell him. The threat against her was serious. She couldn't make any more mistakes.

Jake turned down an unfamiliar side street.

"We're not going to my house?" she asked.

He grunted. "It's not safe. They know where you work; we have to believe they know where you live. You'll stay with me until we find these guys." He twisted his grip on the steering wheel, his knuckles going white.

"Okay." She pursed her lips. "Well, this is one way to find out if we can live together. A trial by fire." She smothered a hysterical chuckle. Diaz had missed his calling. He should have been a matchmaker.

Helping couples find love while threatening their lives. It had worked for her and Jake.

He reached over and grabbed her hand, squeezing. "We'll find these guys." His voice was full of determination and promise.

Caroline wanted to believe him. She probably did believe him, but at the moment she felt too tired to even care.

They pulled into the driveway of a neat two-story townhouse. Another SUV pulled into the space next to them and a vintage muscle car parked behind. Caroline's eyes widened as his fellow squad members climbed out and filled the driveway. "I know you guys have to synchronize your watches and all that, but everyone arriving at the same time is very impressive."

"They followed us from the police station." Jake slid out of his seat and walked around the front of the vehicle. He nodded to his friends before opening her door.

"Caroline." Ryan pulled her into a bear hug. "How are you holding up?"

She fought against the burn in the back of her eyes. "I'm fine. Jake saw the shooter in time." Jake might have seen him, but the memory was a blur in her mind. A figure in dark clothes. That was it. She couldn't even tell if it had been a man or a woman. She'd always thought she was the type of person who paid attention to her surroundings, but she hadn't even seen the gun that had been pointed at her.

A tremor went through her body. The other guys were quick to come give their own brotherly hugs before Jake shooed them off. "Let's get inside," he said, and hurried her to the front door.

She had an impression of high ceilings and sparse, orderly décor before Jake drew her up the staircase. It was as though he lived in a staged home, and Caroline wondered if all military men were as averse to clutter.

"I'll be right down," he called to his friends. "I'm going to get Caroline settled."

"There's really not much to settle," she said as she stepped into his bedroom. "I don't have any clothes with me. Or my computer. Or a toothbrush." She tossed her purse on the bed and followed it down. "I'm settled."

Jake knelt before her. He rubbed his hands lightly over her thighs. "I know you said you didn't need medical attention, but I want to give you a quick check over. I tried not to crush you, but I tackled you pretty hard." He slid his hands over her hips. Tucking his fingers under the hem of her sweater, he gently slid it up and over her arms. He nudged her up off the bed and pulled her skirt down, helping her to step out until she was bare before him except for her underwear.

He skimmed his fingertips over her ribs, along her arms. She hissed in a breath when he pressed his lips to a particularly ugly bruise on her thigh. "I'm sorry, sweetheart."

"It could have been worse." She swallowed. "I could be dead." The image of the stark hole in Brent's head flashed through her mind. The purple marks on her ribs could have been gaping flesh. Instead of her blood gathering to form bruises, it could have been splashed across the lobby of her office building.

Her body trembled. "I could be dead," she repeated. "If you hadn't—"

Jake pressed his finger to her lips and rose to standing. Gently, he tugged her shaking body into his and ran his palms up and down her back. "But I was there. You're alive and you're going to stay that way." His fingertips dug into her skin. "You're freezing. Come on." He led her into the bathroom and started the shower. He stripped out of his clothes then helped her with her remaining bits.

As the water heated, Jake kissed her cheeks, her jaw, her eyelashes, making her feel precious and loved. Steam was billowing from over the top of the shower door before they stepped inside.

He put her back to the spray and her front to his chest. They stood there, Jake just holding her as she trembled. "It's okay, Caroline." Jake pushed her hair out of her face. "You're safe." He brushed his thumb at the trail of tears rolling down her cheeks.

She wrapped her arms around his waist, holding tight. She hadn't even realized that she'd been crying, but now that she'd started, it felt like the tears would never stop. "Why is this happening to me?" Her voice warbled.

Jake pressed his lips to her temple. "I don't know. The world isn't fair. Shit happens to good people all the time. This time it happened to you."

She closed her eyes and sank against his body. Wasn't that the truth? But if she'd never been on the boat, if she'd never been shot at and had to jump into the middle of the ocean and swim for her life, if none of those things had happened she would never have known what it felt like to have Jake's arms wrapped around her. To have him smile at her. Move inside of her.

It was a doozy of a trade-off. If she survived, it would be worth it.

She ran her hands across the muscles of his back. He was so warm, so alive. They'd known each other for such a short time, but she couldn't imagine her life now without him.

She raised her head, her mouth seeking his. She wanted to taste his vitality, wanted to feel it down to her bones. Against all odds she was still alive. Because of this man.

His lips were warm but still beneath hers. "Kiss me," she whispered.

He tugged on a lock of her hair. "This might not be the best time. You've had a shock."

She dug her teeth into his bottom lip, turning his words into a groan. "I'm alive," she said. "And I want to feel alive. I never feel more so then when I'm in your arms." She trailed kisses to his ear, sucked his lobe into her mouth. "Then when you're inside me."

He slid his hands down her back and cupped her bottom. "You sure?"

Wrapping her arms around his neck, she jumped, knowing he'd catch her. She wrapped her legs around his hips and took his mouth. When they finally pulled apart, they were breathless.

She nodded. "I'm sure."

Jake spun and pinned her body against the cold tile wall. He smirked at her squeal. "Don't worry." He lifted her a couple inches, high enough so he could lower his head and draw her nipple into his mouth. "I'll warm you back up."

And he did. In under five minutes she couldn't remember that she had ever been shot at that day. She could barely remember her name.

His name, however, was very familiar. "Jake," she moaned.

He swiveled his hips again, his coarse hair teasing her clit as he thrust inside her. He slapped his palm against the tile as he slammed inside her again. He gripped her butt with his other hand, holding her aloft. His eyes slid closed. "Fuck, you feel so good. So goddamn hot and tight. This is what I want my heaven to be."

A forever with Jake. That sounded pretty damn good to her, too. She sank down on his length, loving the way he filled her. She clenched the muscles of her core and smiled at his muttered curse. Loved the way she could bring him to his knees.

Jake opened his eyes. The jade color seemed electric under the bathroom lights, and his intense gaze sent sparks right through her body. He dug his fingers into her ass and pistoned into her. He fucked her with a single-minded determination. Like she was the only thing in the world that mattered. He fucked her like a man on a mission, his goal being her total capitulation.

Her heart squeezed. She wanted to look away but couldn't. He wanted everything from her, and she didn't know if that was something she could give. "Jake...." Her voice broke.

He pounded into her harder. Faster. "Give over, sweetheart. I've got you."

And he did. When she threw her head back, his hand was there to protect it from the hard tile. When her legs shook, he held onto her, never letting her fall.

She pushed her fears to the back of her mind, and just let herself feel. Tomorrow she could worry about forever. It was only this moment that mattered.

Her body coiled tighter. Her breath grew choppy. Her nipples scraped against his chest with each thrust. With a cry, she curled forward and sank her teeth into his shoulder as she came.

Waves of ecstasy hurtled through her body like a tsunami. Her sheath clamped down so hard Jake had to still, unable to push through her clenching muscles.

"Jesus. Fuck." He shuddered, and wet heat painted her walls. Her body milked his cum, wanting every drop of his essence.

Jake staggered, swore, and sank down to sit on the tiles. His chest heaved beneath hers, his breath panting across her neck. They stayed there, Caroline covering him like a blanket, until the water started to chill.

Jake wrapped his hand around her wet hair and pulled her head back. He took her mouth, sliding his tongue across hers in an act of possession. "Wow," he said.

Caroline snuggled into him. "Right back at you," she said with a lazy grin.

Jake reached up and turned off the water. "You're cold again."

"Just my back." She wiggled. "Everything else is still toasty."

He stilled her with a groan. "Sweetheart, I've got to go down and talk to my guys. You keep doing that, and we're never leaving the bathroom." He helped her off of him and stood. Reaching outside the shower door, he grabbed a towel and rubbed it over her skin until she was pink and dry. He quickly toweled himself off before stepping into his bedroom and heading to his closet.

"Why don't you rest," he said. "I'll make some soup and bring it up to you later."

Memories of all the times she'd brought her mom soup in bed flashed across her mind. Her post-coital Zen wavered. She didn't want to be an invalid with Jake tending to her. Not unless she really needed the tending. "I'm fine."

She kissed his cheek as she walked past to pick up her clothes. She wrinkled her nose. She'd lain on the elevator floor in them. She really didn't want to put them on again.

Jake tossed a pair of sweats next to her on the bed. "Wear these until I have someone go pick up some clothes from your house."

Grateful, she pulled the sweats on, rolling the cuffs at the ankles and wrists multiple times. Not the most flattering of outfits, but it would work until she got her own clothes.

"Seriously, get some rest." Jake pressed his lips to her temple.

The bed did look awfully tempting, even with its complete lack of pillows. How did Jake survive with only the two? She shook her head. Not important right now. "Look," she said, "I know I'm not some commando like you guys, but I want to help. I want to at least be in on the planning stage of how we're going to go about protecting me. It's my life."

Jake opened his mouth, but she stared him down, planting her hands on her hips. "I'm not going to be some damsel-in-distress, lounging around while you guys do all the work of saving me."

He sighed. "I'm not going to win this one, am I?"

"Definitely not."

He shrugged. "Okay. I don't like it, but you have a right to be involved." He headed for the door. "But if you ever want to be more damselly, let me know. I don't mind playing the white knight." He looked back at her, waggling his eyebrows. "There might even be costumes."

She laughed, following after him. She only stumbled twice on his sweatpants as the cuffs unrolled, and she counted that a victory when she made it to his living room unscathed.

The guys had already raided his kitchen, and bags of chips and bowls of salsa were scattered across the coffee table.

Jake dragged Chris from a lounge chair, replacing him with Caroline. He pulled the blanket from the back and draped it over her body. "There's no rule that you can't be comfortable while we plan."

Well, that was true. She snuggled under the blanket and reclined the chair a bit. She rested her head on the soft leather.

"We've already set up shifts for full protection detail," Tony said. "We're pulling in guys from some of the other squads to help. As long as they don't get called out on a mission, they're all available."

Jake nodded. "Any news on the shooter yet?"

Ryan shot a look at Caroline. "The plate you gave us was confirmed stolen. The vehicle was an older model, without any GPS capabilities. I'm still trying to gather camera footage to see if we can track them that way."

Jake nodded, crossing his arms over his wide chest.

Caroline licked her bottom lip. Jake was really sexy when he was in his take-charge mode. She yawned, just remembering to cover her mouth. She slid down another inch on the recliner.

She should probably get more involved in the discussion. Ask some questions. But she could think of absolutely nothing to say. Her eyes slid shut. After all, these men were professionals. Protecting people was actually in their job description.

Her last thought before falling asleep was that being in Jake's house, with his squad around her, was the safest place she could be.

Chapter Seventeen

JAKE LET HIS FRUSTRATION pound out through his fists as he pummeled the boxing bag in the base gym. He and his guys were the only ones using the place, and the tension in the room was palpable.

Ryan held onto the bag, the only thing keeping it from tearing from its bolts. "Cool it, man," Ryan said. "Got to save some of your energy for Caroline tonight." He smirked.

Jake's eyebrows slashed together. He put everything he had into his next punch, and Ryan fell back several steps. "Don't talk about Caroline that way," Jake ordered. He caught the towel Tony tossed to him and wiped the sweat from his face and chest.

"We all like her, Psych. You know that?" Tony stacked his kettle bell with the rest of them. "And we've got her covered," he continued. "Right now, two guys from Delta squad are positioned outside your house. Nothing is getting past them."

"I know." Jake balled up the towel and tossed it towards a bin. It landed on the edge and stayed there. "But it's driving me crazy that I can't be with her when she's under threat. That I can't fix this for her."

"We'll fix it." Chris dropped from a pull-up bar and mopped his chest with his T-shirt. "No one's going to hurt your girl."

The muscles in the back of Jake's neck, the ones that seemed to have turned to stone ever since he'd seen that man pull a weapon on Caroline, slowly began to relax. He was lucky. When things got rough, most men didn't have a group of highly-trained Marines at their side.

He nodded. "I want to finish this. I don't want Caroline living in limbo." Jake paced, running through the information they'd gathered again. It wasn't enough. "We need to track this Diaz's boat. He has to get food and supplies. If he's not docking at a harbor then he sends tenders in. Viper," he said, turning to Tony, "can you check all the harbors within 100 miles from here?"

Tony nodded. "On it."

Travis bent his arm over his head, stretching his triceps muscle. "Maybe he's not on his boat anymore. Hell, he could be back in South America and just left his lackeys to clean up."

"He's staying close." Jake shook his head. "I can feel it. But you're right. He might not be on his boat.

Hawk," he said to Ryan. "Can you do some more of your computer juju? Check for any big spenders at hotels within a 100-mile radius. If he's the son of Cristian Diaz, he's not living frugally. There'll be large hotel bills, women coming and going."

"If he's staying in North Carolina, I'll find him," Ryan said.

"Skee," Jake said, turning to Travis. "Can you go hard into this Brent character's background? If we know how he hooked up with Diaz, we can use the same contacts to find the bastard."

Travis nodded. "Done."

"I can set One Shot up on some databases that will help with his information gathering," Ryan said, jerking his chin at Travis.

Jake nodded. He turned to the last member of the squad. "Chris."

The man huffed. "It's not fair that Travis has two nicknames while I still don't have one. It's times like this I really want a call sign."

Ryan smirked. "When you fuck up bad, a name will come. We're just waiting for the perfect insult."

Jake gripped the back of his neck. He knew the guys used humor to get through tough moments. He'd done it, too. But it was Caroline's safety they were discussing. Now, he just found it annoying.

"Chris," he said a bit sharply. "I want you on point for Caroline's security. Make sure she's never alone."

Chris nodded, his face going solemn. "I've got her," he said. "No one is going to get through us."

Jake dragged his fingers through his hair. He'd convinced Caroline to take several days off from work, but eventually she'd have to get back to her life. And protecting her outside of his home would be that much harder.

Their SOO, Captain Price, strode into the gym. "Skinner." He bobbed his head at the door. "We need to talk."

Jake followed him out into the hallway. "What is it, sir?" Dread pooled in his gut. They couldn't leave on a mission now. He couldn't leave Caroline.

Price pointed to the gym. "You guys discussing the Caroline Carter situation?"

Jake ground his back teeth. Caroline wasn't a situation. She was a woman with a life that needed protecting. She was quickly becoming a major part of *his* life. "Affirmative."

"Then I came at the right time," Price said. "We received information from the D.E.A. They want to take the elder Diaz down by trying to flip the son against the father. They've been made aware of the situation here, and they want to work together."

"We have two conflicting priorities." Jake crossed his arms over his chest. "Their goal is to arrest Diaz. Mine is to protect Caroline at all costs. The two could come into conflict." Because he sure as shit wasn't going to risk Caroline's life attempting to take Diaz in alive, not when his quick death would keep her safer.

Price tilted his head. "Understood. We protect our own here. Uh, this woman, Caroline Carter. She is one of ours now, isn't she?"

Jake swallowed, his throat thick. "Yes sir. She's ours." Which meant that she was his, and nothing sounded better to Jake than Caroline belonging to him.

"I'll inform the head of the DEA investigation of our cooperation." Price gripped Jake's shoulder. "And of our priorities. Ms. Carter's safety comes first."

"I want point on Caroline's security." Jake stared hard into Price's eyes. "That's not negotiable."

The SOO arched an eyebrow.

Jake was pressing his luck speaking to his commanding officer with that tone. He also knew he'd be forgiven. Price was a good guy, and family was family.

The small scar that bisected Price's lips twisted with the man's smile. He shook his head. "Have you and your men in the meeting room in thirty. Let's take this bastard down, fast and hard." Price turned and strode down the hall.

"Oorah," Jake said softly. He turned back to the gym, feeling more hopeful than he had in days.

Chapter Eighteen

CAROLINE SLAPPED THE BLADE down, a chunk of bell pepper bouncing from the cutting board and onto the counter. She picked it up and placed it with its brethren. One thing about Jake's kitchen, he had damn good knives. Everything else about his kitchen was woefully lacking.

One frying pan. One. A half-melted spatula. A cast iron pot that strained her muscles to lift. For someone who liked to cook, like she did, it needed some definite upgrades.

"With a little bit of silicone, we can stitch those bricks together so the wall will be stable." Chris tilted his head. "We'll also have to dig a channel to secure the bottom bricks in. And...."

Caroline tuned out the rest of his words. Another thing Jake's kitchen lacked was peace and quiet. She liked Chris. She did. But ever since he'd come back from her house with a big bag of her clothing and toiletries, he hadn't shut up about the defects in her backyard retaining wall.

Was this a guy thing? Or was it down to both Jake and Chris being Marines that they thought that her two-foot decorative wall should be able to withstand a missile attack? How Chris had been able to sniff out the shortcuts she'd taken building her wall when he was supposedly just picking up her belongings was beyond her.

Maybe Jake had told him. Regardless, she understood now why her friend Sam found Chris annoying.

"—A now involved, this has become a formal op. So—"

Caroline's hand paused, reaching for a stalk of celery. "What was that?" she interrupted. "A formal op?"

Chris pulled open the refrigerator door and bent to look inside. "Yeah, with the DEA now involved, we've been given the go ahead to make this a formal operation for our squad. So you can sit back, relax, and it'll all be over soon." He pulled out a can of soda and popped the top. "I know you're going stir crazy."

"That has strong 'lay back and think of England' vibes." Caroline narrowed her eyes. "I am a fairly competent woman. I want to be involved."

Chris leaned against the counter. "I get that, I do. But I'm trained in intelligence. Jake in advanced special operations. Ryan and Travis in advanced communications and special weapons. And Tony provides us with trauma management. Not to be a dick, but what are you bringing to the team? Righteous anger?"

Caroline stabbed the air between them with the knife. "Do not discount the power of righteous anger." But her heart sank. He was right. She was the rescueé here, not the rescuer. She had to deal with that.

Chris's phone buzzed. He pulled it from his back pocket and checked the message. "Jake's home. That'll be him coming through the door in a minute."

Moments later, Caroline heard the front door open.

Jake strode into the kitchen, his face brightening when he caught sight of Caroline. "Hi, sweetheart." He took the knife from her hand before bending down to brush his lips across hers. "How was your day?"

"Boring," she said.

"Hey." Chris placed his hand over his heart. "That hurts. Here I'd thought we'd become besties."

Caroline threw a chunk of pepper at him.

He snatched it from the air and popped it in his mouth.

"Your friends are something special," she said to Jake.

"Special amazing," Jake said, "or special needs?"

"Ha ha." Chris pushed off the counter and headed for the doorway. "I'll see you later, Caroline. When you get back home, I'll come over and help you with that wall."

Pain throbbed in her temple. "What? No. I—"

Jake patted her shoulder. "I'll be right back. I'm going to see Chris to the door." He fell in after his friend. Soft voices came from the entry before the door snicked opened and closed again.

Caroline loaded up a crock pot she'd dug out of Jake's garage. Vegetables, chicken, and broth went in, followed by a whole lot of cheese.

Jake wrapped his arms around her waist from behind. "What are you making?" he asked.

"Chicken and cheese casserole."

"Looks like a lot of food." He picked out some shredded cheddar and popped it in his mouth.

Caroline put the lid on and set it for three hours. "Guys have been coming and going here all day. I want to be sure there's enough."

Jake turned so his back was to the counter. He pulled her back against him so she rested against his body. "It's just the two of us tonight." His agile fingers found a knot right above her shoulder blade and began massaging it away. "Relax, this will be over soon."

"I'm getting tired of people telling me to relax," she grumbled. But she dropped her head forward so Jake could work on her upper back and neck.

"The DEA has become involved. I just had a meeting with the agent in charge of the operation. He seems competent."

Caroline barked out a laugh. "Competent? That's a word someone uses when they have nothing else nice to say. You don't like the guy?"

Jake dropped his chin to her shoulder. "You're getting to know me well." He sighed. "In point of fact, I didn't like the guy. But I don't have to like him, not as long as he gets the job done." He tucked a strand of her hair behind her ear. He kissed the patch of skin beneath her earlobe.

Her heart fluttered, but she cleared her throat and forced herself to stay focused. "What did he have to say? What's the next move?"

"He's directed one of his undercover agents to start asking about making a big purchase. A purchase too big for the local dealers. He thinks the lure of that amount of money will draw Diaz out of hiding."

Caroline frowned. "Someone offering to buy an amazing amount of drugs just as Diaz is wanted for a murder?" She shook her head. "He'll know it's a trap."

"The DEA agent has been undercover for a long time. He's made connections who trust him." Jake slid his hand down her arm and entwined his fingers with hers. "The agent in charge, one Bob Beaver, if you can believe it, thinks this has a good chance of working."

Caroline nodded. This was good news. A path out of this mess. She should be relieved. But she still felt jumpy, unsettled, and would stay that way until Diaz was behind bars.

"How long 'til that casserole's ready?" Jake asked.

"Not for several hours." She looked at the clock over the oven, her eyebrows drawing together. "You're not hungry yet, are you? It's only three in the afternoon."

"No, I'm not hungry. I just want to make sure we have time for other things."

Caroline turned, her breasts brushing against his chest. "Staff Sergeant Skinner, were you hoping to come home to a little"—she wiggled her hips—"afternoon delight?"

Jake patted her bottom. "Why, Miss Carter, you have a dirty mind." Walking backwards, he pulled her from the kitchen and into his living room. "And for once, that was not what I was thinking."

"Really?" she asked dryly. She found it hard to believe that she'd been thinking about sex when he hadn't. Although, with the way Jake moved, her thoughts were frequently turned toward the bedroom. Or the kitchen counter. Whatever was handy.

"Truly." He shot her a look full of innocence and bullshit. "I had much purer amusements in mind. I thought," he said, kneeling by his entertainment center and opening the door at the bottom, "that we could use the time before dinner to play a couple of games. Help take your mind off things." He pulled out a stack of board games. From the browned and bent cardboard boxes, they looked like they'd been with him since childhood.

He placed them on the coffee table. There was Monopoly, Battleship, and even a Candyland, but it was a Scrabble box he held aloft. "Ready to test your linguistic skills, Miss Carter?"

Caroline arched an eyebrow. "You'll risk playing Scrabble against an English major?" she said jokingly. Then she shrugged. "Or at least half an English major."

He stepped close, the corner of the box nudging her belly. He cupped her cheek, running his thumb along her lower lip. "For you," he said, his eyes turning serious, "I'd risk anything."

Her stomach quivered. This man. He made it so hard to keep her head. She was almost embarrassed at how quickly she'd fallen.

Perhaps she shouldn't be too hard on herself. He was a Raider, after all. Trained to get over walls. Breach defenses. It was no wonder she'd lost the battle.

She grabbed the board game and sauntered to the couch. "Get ready to have your ass handed to you, Skinner."

"A competitive streak?" He stalked after her. "I like it. How about we make this game more interesting?"

She plopped down on the cushion and pulled the lid off the box. "What did you have in mind? A dollar a point?"

"Nothing so boring." He grabbed a chair and placed it across the coffee table. He sank down onto it and leaned forward, resting his elbows on his knees. His gaze locked with hers. "The only words we can make have to be dirty." He smiled, slowly, wickedly. "And the winner gets to try out each and every one on the loser after the game."

Chapter Nineteen

THE RAIN CAME DOWN slow and steady. Jake peered through his scope, the figure in the center outlined in shades of green and black. The DEA's undercover agent stood in the corner of the parking lot of *Vivace*, a high-end Italian restaurant on the river in downtown Jacksonville.

Jake was positioned on the roof of a clothing store next door. He fingered the handle of his Ka-Bar, the only weapon he was allowed to carry tonight. Technically, the Marines had no law enforcement authority stateside. He felt oddly naked without a sidearm.

His earpiece crackled. "Anyone know if this restaurant is any good?" Travis murmured. "It smells good." Skee was in position by the kitchen door around the side, and he'd been moaning about missing dinner all night.

"It only has 3.8 stars on Yelp," Ryan said. As their communications critical skills operator, he was the lucky bastard who got to sit in the DEA van out of the rain, helping to monitor all the audio and video feeds their cameras were capturing.

Tony and Chris were back at Jake's townhouse, watching Caroline. Jake had been torn, leaving her, but he trusted his friends to take care of her.

"I'm hungry." Travis grunted. "3.8 stars will do for me after this is over. What do you guys say? Italian for dinner?"

Jake pressed his microphone against his throat. "Will you focus?" he hissed. "We're not here to fill our stomachs."

It had taken a couple of days, but the DEA's undercover agent had finally gotten a bite. Diaz wanted to meet. A three-million-dollar purchase tended to garner attention.

But Jake didn't like the setup. A light in the parking lot was out, casting shadows over most of the lot. And asking the agent to wait outside? Why wouldn't Diaz want to meet inside the restaurant?

The front door to *Vivace* swung open, and a couple stepped out. They huddled together under the awning until the man popped open an umbrella. They hurried to their car, holding each other tightly.

Jake's fingers ached, and he relaxed his grip on the scope. This was just another mission, he told himself. He'd been in similar positions all over the world. Just because this time it was Caroline's life in the balance, that didn't mean—

He ground his teeth. That was all bullshit. Of course, this was different. He'd been trained to box his emotions up, get the job done, and he would, but he couldn't deny that his heart pumped a little bit faster than in any other op. His muscles tensed with the urge to take action.

Perhaps it was a good thing he wasn't carrying. With Caroline threatened, his finger was feeling awfully twitchy.

Rain droplets plopped onto his back. A pool of water was gathering around him on the roof. He barely noticed the damp.

A group of four people in their early 20s jogged up the paved path by the river and hurried towards the front door, laughing at the rain. As they opened the door to enter the restaurant, the figure of a solitary man came out.

The man paused on the threshold under the awning, adjusted his hat, then moved towards the undercover agent. They strolled to a low wooden fence that separated the pathway with the bank of the river.

"Do we have an ID?" Jake muttered.

"Similar height and build to Diaz," Ryan said. "We don't have a good look at his face."

"Who the hell wears a fedora nowadays?" Travis asked.

"Rich assholes who can afford to be eccentric." Ryan cursed. "Hold up, we're getting audio interference."

Jake focused on the pair. "Can anyone verify it's Diaz?"

"Negative." Ryan mumbled something to an agent in the van. "Okay, audio's clear, but he's being cagey. I think he knows we're listening."

Jake gripped the lip of the roof. Ryan and the DEA agents in the van had access to the undercover agent's microphone, but he and Travis were deaf. It was frustrating as hell.

"The suspect will neither confirm nor deny his identity," Ryan murmured. "He's a coy bitch, and the fucking UA isn't giving us any hints. He did get a picture of Diaz?" he asked someone in the van.

Jake ignored the angry reply. The Raiders would sometimes work with other special operation forces, but that was other military. Working with civilians, even if they were law enforcement, wasn't something he hoped to do again. Perhaps the assessment was unfair, but if felt like amateur hour with these guys.

Jake scanned the parking lot and surrounding environs but nothing else was moving. The rain was keeping people away tonight, and for that he was grateful.

"It's going south, boys," Ryan muttered tersely. "DEA is moving in."

The door to the van slid open and four men spilled out. Each agent wore body armor and carried Glock 22s. They crept towards the two men, keeping to the shadows.

"Shit." Travis moved from his position, coming into view at the front of the restaurant. "We've got company."

The two rear doors of a darkened sedan swung open. The back hatch of an Escalade rose. Dark figures crept out from the vehicles. They raised semi-automatic rifles to their shoulders and aimed at the approaching agents.

Fuck. Jake dropped his scope, gripped the edge of the roof, and swung his body up and over. He hung for a second before dropping to the ground in a crouch.

Gunfire rang across the parking lot. The DEA agents took cover. The UA struggled with fedora-man.

Jake assessed the situation in an instant. Without firepower, he and his men offered little help to the agents. But he could get Diaz.

A man in camo crept from the shadows of *Vivace* and slid up behind one of the drug dealer's shooters. The shooter went down, and his friends didn't even notice.

Jake smiled grimly. He took it back. Even without firearms, his men were deadly. He didn't wait to watch Travis take down another perp. His focus was on the man wrestling with the undercover agent.

"I'm going for Diaz," he told his friends before circling around the parking lot and heading for his target.

Ryan huffed. "The op's gone FUBAR. Watch your back, from both friendly and unfriendly fire."

Keeping low, Jake made his way towards the river. The undercover agent stumbled, went down, and the man in the fedora darted along the pathway.

Jake forgot about stealth. He went into a full sprint, chasing after the man. He hit him in front of an ice cream shop, the light from the large windows falling on the asshole's surprised face a second before Jake tackled him.

They went over the wood railing of the border fence, hit the muddy bank, and rolled down to the river.

A loud boom sounded just as they hit the water, and Jake felt a horse-kick to his abdomen.

He reached for the man's weapon hand and bent his wrist backwards. The man screamed and dropped the pistol. It took less than two seconds to place him in a chokehold. Jake dragged him back to the bank.

Ryan hopped over the railing and slid down the mud wall. He helped Jake haul the guy up to the pathway.

"You okay?" Ryan looked him over, his sharp eyes taking in the hole in Jake's vest.

Jake pressed his hand to the Kevlar, the tip of his forefinger feeling the flattened metal disk. He was going to be sore as hell for the next couple of days, but nothing he couldn't handle. "Fine." Pressing his knee to the man's back, he pulled a plastic restraint from his pocket and bound his wrists. He patted him down before rolling the man to his side.

"Sit rep?" Jake asked. He scanned the parking lot but didn't see any active fighting. It had gone quiet except for the soft lap of the river.

"Perps surrendered. DEA arresting them now."

"Injuries?"

"Minor, though an ambulance is being called for one of this asshole's friends." Ryan toed the guy at their feet.

The man started chuckling.

Jake squatted next to him. The fucker's fedora was in the bottom of the river, and the light from the storefronts illuminated his face.

It wasn't Diaz.

"Something funny?" Jake asked.

"You guys all out here." The man smirked. "Looking for a ghost. But while you're here, who's watching your girl?"

Before thinking better of it, Jake's fist connected with the guy's face. A satisfying spray of blood shot from his mouth.

Ryan pulled him back. "Caroline is fine. Chris and Viper are with her. I've been checking in with them regularly. He's just trying to mess with your head."

Jake stood, taking deep breaths. He looked down at the piece of filth at his feet. The man was still grinning even though his teeth and lips were smeared red with blood.

"I know." Jake gripped the back of his neck. His gut churned and his feet itched to race back home.

With a sigh, he grabbed the goon's arm and dragged him to his feet. Ryan took his other arm, and they marched him to the parking lot.

Jake had known several targets who'd tried to fuck with his mind. They'd enjoyed trying, but trying was all they'd accomplished.

The trouble was, this time, it was working.

Chapter Twenty

CAROLINE RECHECKED HER SPREADSHEET, forcing her mind not to wander. Jake had set up a mini office for her in his guest bedroom, but it was still hard to focus. Shouts erupted from the living room, and she blew out a breath. Chris must have beat Tony in the video game they were playing.

Tony had brought the game system over and tried to teach Caroline how to play, but she'd quickly excused herself, claiming work.

Which was true. If only she could motivate herself to get it done. Rolling her neck, she turned back to her computer screen.

Her boss had been very understanding of her working from home. Which was lucky for him, because Caroline had a sneaking suspicion that if he had given her grief about it, he would have received a visit from Jake. And not the fun kind.

She bounced her pencil against the desktop. Especially considering the mood Jake had been in the last couple of days. She usually only saw him at night, but even then, when he first got back home, he was quiet, intense. What she imagined he was probably like when he was out on a mission.

And now she was the mission. She did what she could to draw him out. Get him to relax. And after twenty minutes or so, she was usually successful. But that watchfulness was always there.

Her computer dinged as a new email popped up in her personal account. The sender's name made her hand pause. Slowly she moved her mouse to open it.

Miss Carter, we received your application regarding the position of assistant librarian. Blah blah, blah. More polite filler and HR speak. Her gaze darted to the bottom of the email.

We would love to set up an interview for some time next week. Please contact us to let us know what works best for you.

"Yes!" Caroline punched her fist in the air. She hadn't realized until she'd received that email just how much she wanted the job.

Even though it paid less. Even though she had little to no experience in the field. But something so small as getting an interview to become an assistant librarian made her feel like she was back on track for her goals from before her mom had died.

She picked up the prepaid phone Jake had insisted she use and dialed his number. She couldn't wait to tell him the news. After all, he was the one responsible for her applying.

The phone rang once, twice, then went to voicemail. She hung up without leaving a message. He was a busy guy. She knew this. She couldn't expect him to answer her all the time.

She called Sam instead. When her friend answered, the news spilled from Caroline's lips.

"That's great." Sam's voice warbled. She sniffed, long and loud.

Caroline stilled. "What's wrong?" Sam never cried.

"Madison is in the hospital." Sam let out a long, shaky breath. "She, she OD'd last night. She still hasn't woken up."

Caroline's stomach bottomed out. Madison was Sam's little sister. Caroline had watched her grow up. She was still just a kid. "Oh god. Why didn't you call me?"

"I know what you've been going through," Sam said. "I didn't want to bother you with my problems."

"You're my best friend." Caroline stood and started gathering her shoes and purse. "You're supposed to bother me. You call me when shit like this happens. I'll be right there, okay?"

"Thanks." Relief colored Sam's voice. "My mom and Frank were here for a little bit, but she couldn't take seeing Madison like this."

Of course, she couldn't. Anger simmered in Caroline's chest. Sam's mom had a hard time handling things under the best of circumstances. She was more interested in sitting on the sofa and drinking herself into a stupor than being a mother to her two daughters. And that left Sam to shoulder the burden.

Even after Sam had moved out, she was still the one to make sure Madison did her homework, got new clothes, and had rides to and from volleyball practice. Caroline had hoped things would get easier for her friend when her mom had remarried, but that had brought a different set of tensions to the family.

"What room are you in?" She wrote down the number on a scrap of paper and shoved it in her pocket. "I'll see you soon."

She hurried down the steps, gripping the banister. "Guys, we have to go," she hollered into the living room.

The TV went silent. Chris and Tony appeared in the hallway. "What's going on?" Chris asked.

Caroline checked her purse, making sure her wallet and keys were inside. "I need to meet Sam at the hospital."

"Your friend is in the hospital?" Chris asked, voice tight.

"No, her sister."

His shoulders slowly lowered. "I'm sorry, Caroline. That's not a good idea."

"Let me ask Jake." Tony pulled out his cell and started texting. His phone buzzed a response a moment later, and Caroline narrowed her eyes.

So Jake had time to respond to his friends but not to her. She inhaled sharply. She'd worry about that later.

Tony slowly shook his head. "Jake says no. It's too dangerous."

Caroline hefted her purse to her shoulder and smiled grimly. "Here's what's going to happen. Either you two take me to the hospital or I call for a ride. If you try to physically stop me from leaving, I'll press charges for false imprisonment and sue you."

The absolute nerve of Jake. The back of her neck went hot. She knew he wanted to keep her safe, but he wasn't her jailor. He didn't get to make decisions for her. She pulled out her phone and opened the ride share app. "Now, are you guys driving me or not?"

Chapter Twenty-One

UPDATE, JAKE TEXTED INTO his phone. He drummed his fingers on his thigh, waiting for the response.

It came in five seconds, but that was still too damn long. *Status quo,* Chris texted back. *Still in hospital room with friend.*

Jake resisted the urge to chuck his phone across the room. Instead, he carefully placed it on the desk in front of him. He and Ryan were in the situation room on base, but Jake wanted nothing more than to join Caroline. "Stubborn, reckless woman," he muttered. Every minute she was away from the safety of his home was a minute off his life.

How did she expect him to provide protection if she wouldn't follow his advice?

He gripped the back of his neck, blowing out a breath. Okay, maybe his advice had been more like an order. And her friend was in need. Logically, he could understand why Caroline had forced the issue and gone to the hospital.

But when it came to her safety, he was having a hard time staying logical.

Ryan smirked. His eyes stayed glued to the computer monitor in front of him. "Lady problems?"

"No problem," Jake bit out. No problem except for the fact that the woman he loved had a homicidal drug dealer after her. One bullet could take her life. He trusted his friends to protect her with their own lives, but if you weren't in a controlled environment, even the best security had holes.

"Uh huh." Ryan leaned forward, squinting at the screen. His tone called bullshit. "That's why I'm single. You get to have fun with women without all the messy feelings."

"I thought you were single because no woman could stand looking at your ugly face long-term." Jake rested his forearms on the back of the chair he straddled. He gave Ryan a considering look. In all the years he'd known him, he'd never seen Ryan with the same woman for longer than two weeks.

Most of his men enjoyed the single life. In their line of work, it was hard to settle down. It almost seemed reckless when you knew you could be leaving a wife a widow if a mission went sideways. And it took a special type of woman to put up with them disappearing for days or weeks on end, having no contact, not knowing if their man was alive or not.

But with Ryan, his aversion to relationships bordered on pathological. "You allergic to commitment?"

"I'm realistic." His lips went white. "I've learned women don't tend to stick around."

Jake frowned. "Caroline—"

"There are exceptions to every rule." Ryan glanced at him from the corner of his eye and shrugged. "You might have hit the jackpot with yours. Doesn't mean every man gets so lucky."

The door swung open, and their Team Chief strode in, Agent Beaver a few steps behind.

Jake stood. "Anything?"

Price crossed his arms over his chest. "Negative."

"No one's talking," Beaver said. "Even facing charges of attempted murder of federal agents and a multitude of weapons infractions, they're keeping quiet. I don't know if they're scared of Diaz or expect a reward from him when they get out of prison in thirty years."

Price rubbed his forehead. "We don't even have confirmation they're Diaz's men."

"It's Diaz." Jake paced the room. "He chose one of his lackeys with a similar build and appearance to confuse the UA just enough not to be able to make an immediate ID."

Jake flexed his hand. The bastard couldn't stay in hiding forever. Even if he escaped back to South America, Jake would find him.

"I might have something." Ryan turned the computer monitor to face them. Long columns of ten-digit numbers filled the screen. He pointed at one of them. "These phone numbers are ones I pulled from the men you arrested last night. This number keeps coming up. It belongs to an attorney, but I don't think he's using it."

"How do you know?" Jake asked.

"According to the guy's social media, he's in Florida right now sipping a piña colada on the beach. The number is currently pinging off local towers, however."

"Where?" Jake bounced on the balls of his feet. Diaz was within his grasp, he could feel it. He might be able to take Caroline out for a celebration dinner toni—

"The phone is in downtown on Third right now," Ryan said.

Jake froze. His blood iced. "Where on Third? Anywhere near Memorial Hospital?"

Ryan turned to his laptop, his fingers flying over the keyboard. He looked back up at Jake, his face grim. "Two blocks away."

Sheer panic raced through Jake's veins before he pulled it together. He grabbed his phone and called Chris as he pushed out the door.

"Yeah?" Chris asked.

"Get Caroline out of there. Now." Jake's feet hit the pavement of the parking lot at a sprint. "Diaz might have found her."

Chapter Twenty-Two

CAROLINE HANDED SAM A paper cup of surprisingly decent cafeteria coffee and settled herself in the chair next to her. "Any changes?"

Sam shook her head, her dark hair spilling over her shoulders. "Maddie still hasn't woken up." The teenager lay still as a statue in the bed, the oxygen and IV tubes connected to her making her look small and vulnerable. "The doctor came by while you were gone. She said Madison should be okay. They think they were able to pump the drugs out of her system in time."

No matter how many assurances the doctor gave, Caroline knew Sam would be a nervous wreck until her sister opened her eyes.

"I've spent too damn much time in hospitals lately," Sam muttered.

Caroline winced. "Sorry about that." She'd been adding to her friend's worry lately, too.

Sam shot her a weak smile. "Try not to get attacked by drug dealers again, okay?"

"Deal."

Sam ran her thumb around the rim of the coffee cup. "I knew she'd been having trouble at school lately. Acting out, getting detention. But I didn't think she was involved in drugs. Seeing how Mom is.... How could she be so stupid?"

Drugs. It kept coming back to drugs. With assholes like Diaz destroying the lives of good people like her friend. She had no way to know if it had been Diaz's drugs Madison had taken, but she was going to lay the blame at his feet anyway. She couldn't wait to see him behind bars.

"What are you going to do?" she asked Sam.

Her friend sighed and slouched deeper into her chair. "Find out how long this has been going on. If this was a one-time thing, or if she's been using for longer. Get her to rehab if she needs it. Ground her for ten years." She huffed out a laugh.

Caroline gripped Sam's hand. Her friend would be the one responsible for all of that. She'd been trying to get her mom into AA for as long as Caroline could remember, with no success. And as a result, she was Madison's primary parent.

Keeping her voice light, Caroline asked, "Where is your mom?"

Sam rubbed her face. "She was here. She couldn't stop crying, and Frank couldn't stop fussing over her. I told her to go home and get some rest. I'll call her when Maddie wakes up."

Sam tilted her head and examined Caroline. "Enough about me. How's house arrest going?"

"A little too much like an actual arrest." Caroline pressed her lips together. "I never would have thought hiding from a drug dealer who wanted to kill me could be so boring."

"Do you get to play with handcuffs at least?" Sam waggled her eyebrows. "Or I bet Jake has those plastic zip-tie thingies."

Caroline's face heated. She and Sam were close, but she didn't feel comfortable talking about her sex life with anyone except the person she was having it with. Even if she did want to brag, just a little. "I don't—"

Chris strode into the room. His gaze cut to Madison, then to Sam before landing on Caroline. "We have to move. Now." He reached for her arm, pulling her out of the chair.

"What?" Caroline dug her heels in. "What's going on?"

"Jake called." He checked his phone. "There's an imminent threat to your security. We have to go." He nodded to Sam. "I asked for a security guard to be sent up to this room. Close the door and stay here with your sister."

Caroline felt the blood drain from her face. "Did I lead him here? I can't leave Sam and her sister if he's coming."

Chris gripped her shoulders, bending down to put his face level with her own. "She'll be safer if we draw you away." He looked over her shoulder at Sam. "I promise, you and you're sister will be safe when we're gone."

Sam plucked Caroline's purse from the ground and chucked it at her. "Go. We're fine. I don't want to have to visit you in the hospital again."

Caroline's stomach clenched with indecision. She hated this. Her problems were spilling over to endanger her friends. But she trusted Jake and his squad. She nodded, and let Chris pull her from the room. "Love you," she shouted back to Sam.

She and Chris passed the elevator and hurried to the stairs. Chris placed her body behind his as he opened the door and checked the stairwell. It was quiet.

They took the three flights down at a near run. The ground floor had a side exit. Chris opened the door, his hand hovering over his waistband.

Tony was already there, his blue muscle car purring at the curb.

Chris yanked open the passenger door, practically shoved Caroline in the back before climbing into the front seat besides Tony. "Let's go."

Caroline fumbled for her seat belt. She had almost locked it into place before Tony took a hard turn and sent her sliding sideways. She pulled herself upright and glared at the back of his head.

"Where are we going? Back to Jake's?"

The guys ignored her. Tony slowed at the four-way stop that led out of the parking lot. A black SUV slowly drove past them.

"Shit," Chris muttered.

Caroline peered out her window but only saw a glimpse of two male figures in the front seat. Nothing about them caused alarm.

Until they pulled a U-turn and sped up behind them.

"What is it with these guys and Escalades?" Chris asked.

Tony didn't even slow down at the next stop sign. "Hold on."

She scraped her hand across the ceiling, searching for an Oh-Shit handle. Nothing. Being in the back seat of a two-door car left her without anything to hold onto as Tony flew through the downtown. Her heart jumped about in her chest like a rabbit, and she didn't know if she was more scared of crashing or of the men behind catching them.

Their car lurched forward as the SUV rammed into its rear fender.

Caroline bit back a scream. Okay, she was more scared of the men behind.

Chris drew a pistol from a holster hidden by his shirt. "I can aim for the tires."

Tony stomped on the gas pedal, the engine roaring with the burst of speed. He took the next turn practically on two wheels. "Hold off," he told Chris. "I can outpace them."

And he did. His car must have guzzled gas like a frat boy downing beer, but it could fly. Tony kept making hard turns and squeaking through yellow lights. The Escalade grew smaller and smaller in the rearview window.

Caroline turned to face forward, taking a shaky breath. Maybe when this was over Jake could set her up with some defensive driving classes. She'd love to learn how to pull some of the maneuvers that Tony had. It could be a fun date—

A dog tugged at its leash, pulling away from the child walking it on the sidewalk. The leash slipped through his hands, and the dog darted into the street, the boy a step behind.

Caroline clamped her eyes shut, her breath stalling in her lungs. She couldn't watch them hit a child. The car slid sideways, making her stomach lurch. The brakes squealed. The car slammed into something, something much harder than a human.

When the ringing of crumpled metal stopped assailing her ears, she opened her eyes, scanning the street. "Oh God, oh God, oh God. Did we hit him?"

Tony turned the key in the ignition and tried to start the car. The engine refused to turn over. "The kid's fine." He pushed open his door. "But we have to move." He took a step, stumbling with a grimace before pushing his seat forward and reaching for her.

Chris scrambled over the hood of the car. He held his gun at his side as he looked down the street. Blood streamed down his face from a cut in his forehead.

Tony wrapped his arm around Caroline's waist and hustled her to the sidewalk. She didn't know if he was helping her or if she was supporting him. His knee butted against his slacks at an odd angle that made her wince in sympathy. She let him lean against her as they lurched down the street.

Chris followed close behind. "We need to find shelter, stat."

Tony grunted. "I can keep moving."

"Sure you can, gimpy."

"You two really should have worn your seat belts," Caroline muttered.

Tony's eyes rolled to the side to give her a look.

"Or maybe have a car that wasn't made before the advent of air bags." Chris hurried in front of them. "There." He pointed at a small bookstore. A bell rang above the door when they entered. The woman behind the counter looked up, her smile slowly fading as she took them in.

"Do you have a rear entrance?" Chris asked. He started dragging a bookcase over to block the window.

"What are you doing?" the clerk said with alarm.

Tony pushed Caroline behind the counter before going to help Chris barricade the store.

The clerk eyed Caroline and took a step back.

"Rear entrance?" Chris shouted.

"Yes." The woman reached for a phone.

Chris tipped a tall shelf, books spilling everywhere, so it leaned against the front door. "Men with lots of firepower are about to show up," he told the clerk. "Leave now."

The woman's eyes darted to the blood on Chris's head. The look in Tony's eyes. She nodded, grabbed her purse, and fled without a word.

Tony limped after her, securing the exit after she left. He pulled out his phone and dialed. "We're at *Behind the Pages* bookstore on Jasper Street," he said. "We're holing up." He locked gazes with Caroline. "Get here fast."

Chapter Twenty-Three

JAKE DROVE LIKE THE devil was after him. When he swung on to Jasper, he saw a large man in a suit trying to kick down the door of the bookstore. Another man stood beside him glancing down the street. Their SUV was parked on the sidewalk, both doors open.

The street was empty except for those two. A group of pedestrians huddled at the end of the block, phones out, recording the commotion.

Jake slammed on his brakes, angling his car behind the other vehicle. Ryan slid from the passenger seat, drawing his sidearm as he moved. The man keeping watch raised his own pistol but didn't have time to take a shot.

Ryan squeezed his trigger. The perp dropped, squealing in pain.

The man's friend turned, eyes going wide. He reached behind his back.

Jake's tackle caught him at the hips. They both went down, crashing into the side of the bookstore.

Jake grabbed him by the collar, pulled his arm back, then dropped the guy in disgust. He was out cold. "Your man still alive?" he asked Ryan as he rolled the limp body over and secured his hands.

"Yep," Ryan said. "Just a shoulder wound."

"Perfect." Jake stepped over to where the man was sitting, leaning against the wall. He dropped to one knee beside him. "Where's Diaz?"

Sweat beaded the asshole's forehead, and his skin had taken on a sickly pallor. He laughed, and anger spiked Jake's body temperature.

He was tired of all these laughing jokers. Tired of seeing the fear in Caroline's eyes. She put on a brave face but there was no denying her terror. He needed to end this so she could get on with her life. With their lives.

He gripped the man's shoulder, found where the bullet had torn into his flesh, and pressed his thumb to the opening. "I'm going to keep asking until I get the answer I want." He dug his thumb a little deeper into the wound, ignoring the girly shriek. "Where's your boss?"

The thug glared at him. "Fuck you."

"Jake." Ryan peered down the street. He holstered his weapon. "Price and Beaver are incoming. Local PD can't be far behind."

Jake nodded. No time to play. He corkscrewed his thumb deep until he could feel a fragment of lead. The man screamed, and Jake almost, *almost* felt bad for him. "This is your last chance before I start adding to your hole collection. Where's Diaz?"

"If I'd known you were so eager to meet me, I would have introduced myself days ago."

Jake whipped his head around. Diaz leaned out of the Escalade, a nine millimeter Beretta trained on Ryan. He stepped fully from the vehicle, a smirk playing around his lips.

Ryan raised his hands, his jaw tight.

Jake gritted his teeth. He couldn't believe he'd let Diaz get the drop on them. He should have checked the vehicle. He'd been so narrow-mindedly determined to save Caroline, he'd forgotten the basics of securing his surroundings.

The muzzle of Diaz's pistol leveled on Ryan's chest. Jake stilled. And his stupidity just might get his friend killed.

Jake dropped the man at his feet and stood to face Diaz. "Joining your men on a kill? A bit reckless, wouldn't you say?"

Diaz raised one shoulder. "Did you think I wouldn't be here to watch your girl die?"

A siren sounded faintly in the distance. Jake took a step to the side, trying to put space between him and Ryan and pull Diaz's focus. And just as he'd hoped, Diaz turned his weapon on Jake. "Your father was smart not to let you take over his cartel. You're too stupid not to get caught."

A blue sedan screeched to a stop at the end of the block. Price and Beaver stepped out, taking up positions behind the car's open doors.

"I'll be okay." Diaz's eyes glowed, like he was having the time of his life. "With the lawyers I have, I doubt I'll even go to trial."

Jake swallowed. There was a chance he was right. The only charge against him that they had any proof of was murder. And for that to stick, Caroline would have to testify, keeping her a target through the trial. Or worse, their government wouldn't even attempt to try him, instead giving him immunity to flip on his father.

Diaz jerked his head to the bookstore. "How long you think you can hide her? It won't be long enough."

No. It wouldn't. Diaz wouldn't leave Caroline alone. He was the kind of man who'd want payback, the kind of man who took his revenge, even if it came years later.

If Diaz was alive, Caroline would never be safe.

Jake straightened his spine. He locked gazes with Ryan.

Ryan nodded.

Jake's fingers twitched. He visualized the movements that he'd practiced thousands of times. He slowed his breathing and waited.

Ryan whistled, the sound short and piercing.

Diaz started, swinging his firearm towards the sound.

Jake lifted the front of his shirt with his left hand, pulled his weapon with his right, and shot Diaz in the side of the head. The man dropped to the pavement, unmoving.

Jake stepped over to the body and kicked the weapon from Diaz's limp hand. He didn't bother checking for a pulse. The hole in the man's head was too big for anyone to survive.

Ryan checked the Escalade. "No one else," he said before moving to the bookstore door. He pounded on it. "We're clear," he shouted.

Agent Beaver trotted up, his face red. Price followed at a more sedate pace.

"We wanted him alive." Price planted his hands on his hips.

"He was about to shoot my friend." Jake re-holstered his sidearm. This was going to be a cluster-fuck of epic proportions. The police would have to arrest him. He'd be processed, possibly face charges.

And none of that mattered. Caroline was safe.

He left his Team Chief arguing with the DEA agent and strode to the door of the bookstore. His back tensed as he waited for Chris and Tony to remove their barricades.

The second they did, Caroline was in his arms.

Jake turned so she wouldn't see the carnage on the sidewalk. He buried his nose in her hair, breathing deeply. His muscles sagged with relief. "It's over, sweetheart."

Chapter Twenty-Four

CAROLINE TUGGED JAKE'S T-SHIRT free from the waistband of his underwear as they tumbled from her bedroom. He finished buttoning his shorts, giving her a wicked grin. "If that's the kind of attention I'm going to get, I think I'm going to enjoy living with you very much."

"You think you'll get that treatment all the time?" She arched an eyebrow. As far as she was concerned, he deserved her attention morning, noon, and night. And lucky for her, it was never one-sided. Jake gave as good as he got.

"Can't you two keep your hands off each other for more than five minutes?" Sam stood at the door leading to Caroline's backyard. She narrowed her eyes, staring at Caroline's head.

Caroline smoothed her hair down. "You should have told me I have just-fucked hair," she hissed at Jake. Turning to her friend, she gave her an innocent smile. "We were, uh, just checking to see if we had enough hamburger buns."

Jake smothered a snort, not looking at all abashed when she shot him a dirty look.

"In your bedroom?" Sam shook her head.

"I, uh, well, you see...."

Jake tucked her into his side and moved them down the hallway towards Sam. "We were trained," he said in her ear, "that when a mark isn't believing your bullshit, it's best just to keep your mouth shut."

Caroline nodded. She could do that. After weeks of multiple interviews with various law enforcement agencies, staying quiet would be nice for a change.

She took Jake's hand and squeezed. The local DA had decided not to press charges, deeming the shooting self-defense. Diaz's men had scattered, at least the ones who hadn't been arrested.

Leaving Caroline finally feeling safe. And ready to move on.

She and Jake followed Sam out to the backyard. Ryan was manning Jake's grill, one of the few additions he'd brought to Caroline's house. He'd sold or donated his furniture, and hadn't owned any artwork, so it had pretty much just been him moving in. Him, his barbeque, and his TV after he deemed hers pathetically small.

Two folding tables were set up next to her small iron patio table. A rowdy game of cornhole was taking place on her lawn. Music played from one of the guy's sound systems.

She stopped on her patio and looked around at her friends. They were here to celebrate Jake moving in. And Caroline's new job at the Swansboro library. It had been her spreadsheet skills that had landed her the job. She would still be working on a computer most of the day, but there would be author signings to arrange, children's events to set up, and decisions on what books the library should buy, as well. She couldn't wait to get started.

All the guys from Jake's squad were there, including Team Chief Price. Tony and Travis had brought dates. Sam had brought Madison, who was currently sitting at a table laughing at something Chris said and looking as healthy and hearty as any normal fifteen-year-old.

Caroline lifted her face to the sun. It was a good day. She leaned her head on Jake's shoulder. She couldn't believe she'd almost missed this because of some stupid personal rule about who she would and wouldn't date.

Her fear had almost kept her from living her best life.

She tucked her fingers into the back of Jake's shorts. She was still terrified for him, doing what he did. She'd asked Sam to come over and stay with her when Jake had been called out on his last mission.

But he loved being a Raider, and she didn't want to stand in his way.

Sam held up her phone. "Say cheese," she told them before snapping a pic.

Chris strolled up holding a bag of chips. "Broadcasting our location to the world again?"

Sam's face went red. "Are you going to bring that up every time I see you?"

Chris shoveled some potato chips in his mouth and shrugged.

"Don't tease her," Caroline said. "She feels bad enough, and besides, it wasn't her fault."

With Diaz dead, some of his men had started talking. And one of the things they'd told the police was how they'd found Caroline that day at the hospital. Knowing she and Sam were close friends, they'd kept track of her friend's social media. When Caroline had gone to the cafeteria for coffee that day, Sam had dropped a quick post saying she was thankful for good friends. Her location at the hospital had been tagged.

"I didn't use anyone's name," Sam muttered.

"Turns out you didn't need to." Chris crumpled the bag and shot it toward the trash can. "Diaz was smart enough to figure it out on his own."

"Enough." Jake used his Element Leader voice, the one that demanded deference from his men and sent a shiver straight down Caroline's spine.

She squeezed his hip. She knew he'd been just as pissed at Sam when they'd learned what had happened, but unlike Chris, he'd gotten over it. The mistake had been unintentional, and no one felt worse about it than Sam.

Tony joined them, holding a brick in his hand. "Caroline, did you know your retaining wall isn't anchored?" He held up the brick. "These are just stacked one on the other, completely loose."

Oh, sweet baby Jesus. Caroline sucked in a breath, her back muscles tensing. "It's fi—"

"I mentioned that to her the other day." Chris took the brick and rolled it over in his hands. "The wall just needs some silicone adhesive. Maybe a better trench to stabilize its base."

Caroline rubbed her temple. "I don't need—"

"I saw some shovels in her garage." Tony checked his cell phone. "There's a hardware store only two miles away. They should have what we need. And it's near an auto supply store. I need some more Bondo for my car. I've almost finished repairing the body."

Chris nodded. "We'll be back soon."

"I don't need you to fix my wall." She planted her hands on her hips.

"Don't worry." Chris waved his hand like it was no bother. "I was raised in construction. I know what I'm doing." He and Tony headed for the gate leading to her driveway.

Caroline stared after them, her mouth hanging open. Irritating, interfering men. Why couldn't they—

"I've got to make sure they buy the right stuff." Jake brushed a kiss over her forehead before trotting after them.

"But...."

"Don't worry," he yelled. "It'll be perfect."

Caroline dropped her face into her hand. She shook her head, her lips curling into a smile. A burst of laughter escaped her mouth.

"I don't get it," Sam said. "What's so funny?"

"I'm getting a new and improved wall, whether I like it or not." She laughed harder. She was living with a man who expected nothing less than one hundred percent effort while she had been content to half-ass her way through life.

It was going to be frustrating. Downright annoying at times.

And so much richer than the life that she'd been living.

Madison walked up to them. "We're out of hamburger buns. Some of them might have gone to feed some birds."

Caroline wiped her eyes. She slung her arms around Sam's and Maddie's shoulders. "I'll text Jake to pick some up."

<<<<<>>>>>

Thanks for reading HUNTED! I've long been a reader of military romance, but this was my first foray into writing it. I had a blast bringing these characters to
life, and can't wait to dive further into these sexy Raiders.

The special forces trained him to face any challenge. She'll test him in ways he never imagined. Corporal Chris Gunn plays hard, fights harder, and hasn't met a woman he couldn't charm. Until her. His life as a Marine Raider would be close to perfect if it wasn't
for the woman who seems tailor-made to provoke him at every turn.
Samantha doesn't have time for BS. Between her job, her checked-out mother, and the little sister whose antics will turn her prematurely gray, she has zero time
for an adult pretender whose ego is only surpassed by his bossiness. And his hotness. Pretending to ignore the Raider while he pushes all her buttons has
become her own personal Olympic sport, and she's determined to take gold.
But when a stalker sets his sights on Samantha, Chris will do everything in his power to protect the only woman who's ever gotten under his skin. If

these two
can stop fighting each other, they just might be
able to stop a threat bent on revenge. And they
might discover that, sometimes, the person you
can't stand
ends up being the one you can't live without.

If you like sexy and fast-paced romances with dom-
inant men and the women who can tame them,
you'll love STALKED. Start reading this steamy romance today!

Also By This Author

Putting Out Old Flames

Under the Christmas Tree

Courting Disaster

All Wrapped Up

Shelter Me

Forever Home

Forever Found

Forever Wild

The Bakeshop at Pumpkin and Spice (with Donna Kauffman and Kate Angell)

A Wedding On Bluebird Way (with Lori Wilde, Janet Dailey, and Stacey Keith)

That Mistletoe Moment (with Cat Johnson and Kate Angell)

About Allyson Charles

Allyson Charles lives in Colorado. She's the author of sexy and funny small-town romances, and steamy and fast-paced military romances. A former attorney, she happily ditched those suits and now works in her pajamas writing about men's briefs instead of legal briefs. When she's not writing, she's probably engaged in one of her favorite hobbies: napping, eating, or martial arts (That last one almost makes up for the first two, right?). One of Allyson's greatest sources of happiness is that she now lives in a city that has a Cracker Barrel.

Allyson Charles also writes steamy historical romances under the name Alyson Chase, and paranormal romances under the name A. Caprice. You can find her at www.allysoncharles.com.

Printed in Great Britain
by Amazon

41335286R00119